Gracious

Gracious

Poems from the 21st Century South

Edited by John Poch
Introduction by Bryan Giemza

TEXAS TECH UNIVERSITY PRESS

This book is typeset in Baskerville MT Pro. The paper used in this book meets the minimum requirements of ANSI/NISO Z39.48-1992 (R1997).∞

Designed by Hannah Gaskamp
Cover designed by Hannah Gaskamp. Image: *Scarlet Branches* by Todd Murphy, used with permission.

Library of Congress Control Number: 2020940629
ISBN 978-1-68283-064-2 (paperback)

Printed in the United States of America
20 21 22 23 24 25 26 27 28 / 9 8 7 6 5 4 3 2 1
Texas Tech University Press
Box 41037
Lubbock, Texas 79409-1037 USA
800.832.4042
ttup@ttu.edu
www.ttupress.org

For David Bottoms

Contents

Introduction

It is a sure sign that an academic discipline has achieved its full maturity when, through theory and much discussion, it disproves the need for its own existence.

This turns out to be true not only in the sciences but also in the humanities and, I might add, a bit ruefully, in the short-lived career of what used to be called "southern studies," an area of enquiry that is endangered if not yet extinct. For a while, it was a going academic concern, defined partly by tensions between scholars at Vanderbilt and the University of North Carolina, and fueled by the convergent, bright-burning talents of a remarkable group of writers. The vibrant capital-S Southern Literature scene among novelists and story writers certainly abetted the visibility of southern poetry, too. Ross White, poet and director of Bull City Press, an important wellspring for southern poetry today, remembers the Chapel Hill hub of the southern writing scene in the '90s much as I do. He told me in a recent email:

> It was a thrilling time to be a student of southern literature. While there was an abundance of dead mules[1] in the work, there was a tremendous energy and pride in being identified as a Southern writer. Doris Betts was at the height of her power, Randall Kenan was just beginning to tear it up, Alice Walker and Clyde Edgerton and Tony Earley and Dorothy Allison were putting on clinics. Poets like Rodney Jones, Kate Daniels, Charles Wright, and Betty Adcock took pride in their southernness, despite its compromises and contradictions. It didn't feel like it was rooted in holding on to a way of life; it felt like it was rooted in having a New York-centric establishment take notice of the fact that there were other states of being.

1 White is referring to the dead mule test, famously posited by Jerry Leath Mills: for some strange reason, southern writers love to reference a dead mule in their work. This circumstance turns out to be weirdly, uncannily, and grotesquely true for many southern writers in the traditional canon (Faulkner, O'Connor, Welty, and Cormac McCarthy, for that matter). The Dead Mule Club, a bar in Chapel Hill, came into being in the 1990s and remains an inside joke, a sly signifier to the southern lit in-crowd.

White joins a long line of excellent southern writers in being uneasy about the southern poet label, and he is quick to acknowledge that this list is "predominantly (overwhelmingly) white." The celebration of Southern Literature as such paradoxically could work to stifle the very diversity it purported to celebrate, even as a new wave of southern writers attempted to pry open the canon. Gifted literary scholars did their part with more expansive southern anthologies and arguably helped prepare the ground for a "Great Awokening" that remained stubbornly evasive to southern and national realpolitik. The party music of a boisterous writing scene was answered by the looming silence of Chapel Hill's Confederate monument on McCorkle Place. White acknowledges, "It'd be tempting to write off that period in southern literature as a move to maintain and preserve white supremacy."

But it would be a mistake to do so altogether. No small part of the excitement of that time was in a rising, if inchoate, awareness. The canon was beginning to understand southernness as otherness, a term from literary theory now so mainstream that many *Gracious* contributors self-consciously use it to explain what southern poetry is. If literary criticism is something of a lagging indicator of what sociologist William H. Sewell Jr. calls moments of eventful transformation, the nineties marked the start of a quarter-century of evolving critical apologetics. Scholars confronted rising awareness of white supremacy and its constant confederate, privilege. The two forces rippled and occasionally blazed through southern literature, yet the question remained: how would supremacy be noticed in scholarly institutions whose very origin stories were steeped in white supremacy? (Would universities remain silent about their Silent Sams?) How would the narrative grow beyond a first generation of southern studies that sometimes wittingly, sometimes unwittingly, permitted nostalgia to cover the whiteness of the southern literary canon?

On the one hand, "old verities" about sense of place, mama's biscuits, and the like were not likely to satisfy anyone for long. And they didn't. Critics pointed out that assertions about southern culture were too often race blind, or else constituted whiteness studies in another guise. The strangeness of the situation could be seen on the segregated shelves of commercial booksellers, which often had separate sections for "Southern" and "African American" literature.

As if the two could ever be disentangled. The only way to cleave the inseparable is by the violence of ideology or deliberate forgetfulness. Erin Belieu's poem, "How We Count In The South," gets at this concept in its portrait of a fallen, postbellum South of feckless white longing, where "Every day is a day before." Shelby Foote observed that white southerners lost the war and "won" Reconstruction by enthroning white supremacy. Similarly, in "Going to the Movies Alone," Ansel Elkins paints a revisionist South especially hungry for national cinematic deliverance, a place where "Everything's gonna be OK. We won." Town squares, and their precarious soldiers facing north, remind us that in a history-sick country it is easier to efface a symbol than to effect meaningful change.

In the circles of scholarship, it was only a matter of time before the moonlight-and-magnolias view of the South became an easy target for the righteous. The resulting show of indignation consumed a decade or two of scholarly energy. I struggled to find the right comparison for it before landing on professional wrestling. You know who is going to be in the ring: the skulking but disguised racist, Mr. Nostalgia, bucking up to Professor Anti-ism, who swaggers on the ropes, all strapped with race, class, and gender. They preen and strut, and each match ends with a more or less satisfying repentance of regional mythologies and the self-serving hierarchies they perpetuate. With Mr. Nostalgia pinned, wailing, to the mat, Dr. Anti-ism could make a show of dealing fake blows while winking at the camera. Books were written and screeds were posted. Reputations were forged.

Of course, everyone knows that pro wrestling isn't real, and the enterprise was well on its way to disproving the need for its existence. You get a sense of where the conversation turned with the title of Michael Kreyling's book, *The South That Wasn't There: Postsouthern Memory and History.* Enter the era of the postsouthern south, when southern studies embraced the idea that the only South to be studied was one of "imaginaries," in the academic term du jour. It led to a new conception of southern studies, named, not very imaginatively, the new southern studies.

However, anyone with her wits about her could drive out the portcullis of a southern ivory tower and down a road and be pretty damn certain that there *was* a South, and she was in it. As William Walsh observes in one of many interesting contributor musings about southern poetry today, "The real South is when you travel thirty miles outside any metro area." What about a post-rural South? After all, the three traditional qualities differentiating the South from the rest of the country—race, rurality, and religion— long since identified by sociologists like John Shelton Reed are still obstinately observable, if less sharply defined, in our time. Each of these factors has proved changeable and yet resistant to broader change. For example, rural attitudes can persist in southern cities, and one need only look at the way election maps correspond to regional attitudes to know that race and religion are still definers.

Even as southern studies wilted away in some of the university quarters where it was once well established and sought out new habitat in places where it hadn't been (for example, in the far-flung sanctuaries of American Studies programs, including some abroad), a third position seemed, sensibly, to emerge, this time out-side of academe. To my lights, it's the epoch where we find our-selves now, and its title might be encapsulated by the online journal, *The Bitter Southerner*. The title has nothing to do with disaffected southerners of the kind who fomented massive resistance when the integration mandate reached Virginia, nor those southerners who saw themselves unfairly lumped in the basket of deplorables and who in consequence helped sweep in a new era of demagoguery. The term "bitter southerner" recognizes that a moonlight-and-magnolias view of the region doesn't get it, and neither does an endless *mea maxima culpa* approach to regional identity. Black, white, native, and other southerners may have disparate grievances but a shared interest, as *The Bitter Southerner* puts it, in "the [South] we live in today and the one we hope to create in the future." All might agree that identifying as a southerner is at best bittersweet, and southerners have increasingly global ways of seeing themselves within a globalized region. Again, poet / publisher Ross White:

> The state of southern literature today feels decidedly less "Southern," insofar as writers from the south are exploring place in a global context. The need for regionalism feels

somehow less severe when we have the literature of a whole world at our fingertips, and with it, a recognition that too many stories were being left out. I think maybe the stories that southerners are telling themselves about southernness are changing, just because the beauty of this place—about which so much ink has been spilled—has brought more people here, and made it a global community. I have loved seeing the redefinition of the south and southernness that's taken place over the last twenty years, the move from "new south" to "new new south."

Here in the new new south, the contradictions remain. Alongside the spirit of invention that defines the South today, Josephine Yu points with wonderful clarity to the enduring sense of loss and unfinished business, the *et in Arcadia ego* for the electricity of her remembered Atlanta art scene: "Yet I often felt a sadness there I didn't understand, a feeling I might attribute now to how much was left unfinished and uncared for." The mingling of activism and creativity is a significant aspect of this new new south ethos, an Atlanta Beltline to encircle the regional mind. It is the Bitter Southerner's perennial call for renewal as the crumbling national post-racial fantasy reminds us that post-post-place is not post-post-race. Grr/race-ious? While I write this, gun rights advocates gather in the former capital of the Confederacy on Martin Luther King Jr. Day.

And by the time I revisited this introduction, George Floyd's death at the hands of police had demonstrated, with terrible clarity, the danger of white silence, and why a national willingness to revisit equity and equality is, for so many, not just a matter of prosperity but mere survival. Floyd's roots in the South show how the unfinishable business of race remains a national problem, and how histories unseen or unacknowledged are repeated. Perhaps the problem with new souths, academic and otherwise, is that they never turn out to be truly new.

Derek Chauvin and George Floyd worked at the same place, in the same role, at different times. It's not a new notion, but to be southern is to recognize what it is to live with the best of enemies and the worst of friends. For example, I knew a woman of considerable religious conviction who was an unrepentant racist. She went more or less blind as she entered her ninth decade, during which her African American caretaker became her best friend, following her in prayer and to the toilet. When it became necessary to point out that her best friend might take offense to the views she routinely aired, she said, "Well, *she's* not black." The South is a place where we like a good freak show, to paraphrase Flannery O'Connor, because we both supply the freaks and—sometimes—recognize them.

John Poch cites Leon Stokesbury's sense of the region's essence: "family, landscape, religion, and some important tension between comedy and heartbreak." Yes. The South is, in a sense, the crucible for American failure (considered the failed aspirations of Reconstruction) while simultaneously a dynamo for cultural invention (Coca Cola, blue jeans, rock and roll) and astonishing self-reliance (consider the long Civil Rights movement, or the way that Gulf Coast communities have responded to the toll of environmental disasters ranging from hurricanes to petrochemical spills).

But if you should find yourself doubting the existence of the region, you might try a "man who fell from space" exercise: what three questions could an alien visitor ask to determine for certain he was in the South? Grimly, you could probably verify with a handful of public health questions, like, What are the rates of obesity, cancer, heart disease, smoking, sexually transmitted illnesses? Adequate insurance coverage? You'd know in a hurry if you were somewhere in the region if the answer to the first set of questions was "high," and the second, "low." You could cut to the chase and simply ask, Are you in the best part of the country? If most of the respondents say yes, there's a very good chance you're in the South. What New Englander or Midwesterner would presume?

Suppose we applied a similar thought experiment to the poems in this anthology. Put differently, how do we know we're in a southern poetry anthology in an era of regional blandification, and where would you put it in on the map? Reflecting deep currents of culture—and befitting one who has made West Texas his home—John Poch's South arguably skews a little to the southwest. "Layover," "Sandhill Crane," "Moonrise," the variations on "Country-Western Singer," and "Dust Devil" suffice to make the point.

More broadly, there are multiple southern tells within the collection. The potential for violence—to self and to others—is a signifier here. We see it reflected in the work of African American poets whose lived experience of southern violence runs deep, in works such as Sean Hill's "Boy" and TJ Jarrett's "My Father Explains the History of Sugar . . . " Cognizant that the South is continuously swept by tides of migration, this anthology offers ambivalent insider / outsider perspectives of various southern ethnicities who question old and presumptively white Protestant narratives of regional identity, offering in return—to borrow from Josephine Yu's title—more accurate representations.

Other regional indicators emerge across poems, too. Loyalty to family and country, even in time of dying; the profound dangers of nostalgia; the desire to escape an earthbound existence; the ferocious claims of motherhood and pretty-is-as-pretty-does southern womanhood; the way that religion won't relinquish its hold on mind or speech or class; the poisonous sweetness of slavery and chattel-based capitalism: all of these become regional markers and emerge in at least leitmotif. In fact, I saw these things before seeing them elegantly confirmed in the appendix. And I could name sets of poems for each of them, but you are likely to find more pleasure in finding them for yourself. If there were no order, the mind, as merrily as a beagle on a scattering rabbit trail, would impose it anyway.

The title of this collection is particularly apt, because grace is the only way to achieve a measure of reconciliation with all of the power and the glory in a region characterized by violent contention and occasional campaigns of genocide—as well as acts of stupendous invention. Although "community" is a much-abused word, we might say community solidarity. Places where narrative still fetches high value, in a region where fecundity encourages every sort of creativity and cover-up. As Natalie Graham's "Intersection" puts it, "As summer persists, / everything exaggerates." Consider those lines in an era of climate change. Already much given to exaggeration, political and otherwise, what does it portend for this South? For global souths? Expansion? Contraction? A new end?

To the extent that they evoke old sense-of-place clichés, these notions won't find much favor in the current version of southern studies. Fair enough. There is every reason to be wary of any kind of regional essentialism. Better to look for what emerges. Studies show that the happiest people on earth socialize for eight (!) hours a day, and there remains a love of talk in the South. Through words we are still working out what can never be worked out.

In a region with a reputational love of words, there's also a great distrust of words. Cormac McCarthy—who, like many of the contributors in this volume, was raised in the South by transplanted parents—wrote about the equivocations of language in a recent essay, "The Kekulé Problem":

> There are a number of examples of signaling in the animal world that might be taken for a protolanguage. Chipmunks, among other species, have one alarm call for aerial predators and another for those on the ground: hawks as distinct from foxes or cats. Very useful. But what is missing here is the central idea of language, that one thing can be another thing. It is the idea that Helen Keller suddenly understood at the well. That the sign for water was not simply what you did to get a glass of water. It was the glass of water. It was in fact the water in the glass.

McCarthy suggests that language is a late arrival to the unconscious and that the two might in fact be inimical. One of John Grady Cole's plainspoken ranch hand aphorisms in *All the Pretty Horses* is, "There ain't but one truth. The truth is what happened. It ain't what come out of somebody's mouth." Granted. But not granite. Poets know better than to come at the truth that way. When words render the unconscious through things, they render the miracle of thought, the great step between a notion and its expression, briefly and mysteriously visible to all. Thoughts and words are not the same thing, so this rendering is something much greater than simple truth or verisimilitude. "One thing can be another."

Why is it that every child understands metaphor and the notion that one thing can be another, including people? It is for want of metaphor that we lose our natural sympathies and become the wrong things, accepting labels as doctors and lawyers and such. In this way, language expels us from the garden of original imagination. We call on the poets and tale-tellers to bring us back and navigate a world made unfamiliar. In "Explaining an Affinity for Bats," Alicia Stallings draws parallels between the poets and the echolocation of bats "Who find their way by calling into darkness / To hear their voice bounce off the shape of things." Often the most we can hope to do is to use words to understand relationships that reveal the pattern inscribing our place in the universe.

What is the moving target in echolocation—the traveler, the world transited, or both? If this introduction at times sounds like an encomium for the academic study of the region, that obituary is undoubtedly premature, since the subject of study is what brings a field to full bloom.

And poetry is our regional white deer (not a white whale, of course). It is the albino deer that shows up from time to time in the piedmont of my native North Carolina, the deer that brings back oldest memory, the deer of rumor and belief, and of the way things are told. The white whitetail, back from presumed extinction, as present as poetry in the popular consciousness and about as rare. But no less needful for it. Full of numinous significance, the white deer are the moment when the familiar becomes unfamiliar and steps into the yard, walks onto the page. The moment when the lovesick stag of Doris Betts's short story "The Ugliest Pilgrim" strides right from the Song of Solomon into the world of the televangelist, blinks, and bolts (the story ends with a protagonist who "plunges through the crowd like a deer through fetterbush," pursued breathlessly by her lover). Yes, poems are our white deer, called up from James Dickey's "The Heaven of Animals":

> To match them, the landscape flowers,
> Outdoing, desperately
> Outdoing what is required:
> The richest wood,
> The deepest field.

Dickey is gone. Sometimes the field is, too. Enter a new dispensation. Ross White says, "Southern poetry is so, so healthy, and southern voices are more prominent than ever before." Amen, inshallah. By some strange new grace, southern poetry leaps on these pages.

BRYAN GIEMZA

Prologue

I don't know what exactly is the South. Part of it might be the strange syntax of this first sentence that seems like a question. The way we talk betrays where we're from. Ending on a preposition or leaving a fragment hanging in thin air. Shifting the emphasis on the usual order of words to create a tone, perhaps one particular to a region. Robert Frost calls this "the sound of sense," although I believe he's specifically talking about New England English. Frost says that "much meaning is carried in tone," and those of us who listen for it know so many examples of how tone varies regionally and is often shaped by a slight shift in the usual order of words. So the South is not just a grouping of geographical states but also a kind of language.

A few years ago, I was asked to write some paragraphs for the *Oxford American* special issue featuring Texas music. I'm no expert in music, but I know a thing or two about the lyric, so I agreed to scratch out a few thoughts. Here is a part of what I wrote for that little essay:

> Texas demands a fierce independence whereas the South hunkers down into a forlorn neighborliness. I feel a shift in consciousness when I leave Lake Charles and cross into the Lone Star State. And when you leave Farwell, drifting past Clovis toward an even drier open space that is the otherworldly Southwest, something else shifts. Let's not even talk about the disappointment Texans feel when they cross north into Oklahoma.
>
> In a place where we have few trees and a lot of wind, I'll risk it and go out on a limb to say that Texas may be a part of the New South. Texas doesn't believe that, but still, there's a common bond. Almost. I think it was Leon Stokesbury whom I first heard define the Southern poem. He thought such a poem likely included a big dose of heartbreak and comic sensibility featuring family, landscape, and religion in varying degrees and combination. I hear these same quirky, dusty, open-sky, heartfelt mixtures

in the songs of Townes Van Zandt, Lyle Lovett, the Dixie Chicks (don't judge), and, more recently, Amanda Shires.

Are music lyrics poetry? Is Texas part of the South? Both of these questions must be answered: Yes. And also, no. It's complicated.

My time growing up in the South from twelve till my early twenties was in general an experience of fine neighborliness. I was a scrawny, lower-middle-class boy who got pretty good grades in school and was decent at sports. I was fairly privileged, no doubt. I can't speak for others (especially those of other races) as to their own social interactions, but I can say that many years later when I moved from the South to Scottsdale, Arizona, for a year, it was a bit of a shock to me that in the grocery store people, in general, didn't look me in the eye and weren't accustomed to a stranger saying "hello, how ya doin'." In fact, many looked at me downright offended, as if I wanted something from them.

What is the South? It's harder than ever to say. Nowadays, people don't often stay put for a lifetime or even a decade. We're mobile, and so few of us are bound to the land as most of our fore-bears were for the last few hundred years here. When our conversations happen at nearly the speed of light over phones, computers, etc., the distance between us evaporates, in a way. Place mostly becomes irrelevant, and region can hardly seem what it was twenty years ago. Friends certainly aren't what they used to be. In the past we had a few, and now we have perhaps thousands whom we might "unfriend" with a click. The South isn't just the land south of the Mason–Dixon Line and east of the Mississippi River, the slave states, Dixie, these southern United States. A Facebook friend sent me an image of a map of the South, and it seemed convincing to me, geographically, and only after I saw the land mass did I notice that the color of the mapping was defined by the popular presence of Baptist churches. Is the South Baptist? Immersion in water rather than sprinkling?

What about race? Is the South racist? Obviously, not all the South. And racism thrives in the North and West, as well. But there is no denying that the South is largely comprised of what were formerly known as the slave states. People who deny Texas is part of the South might forget that Texas was a slave state.

Despite the recent removal of Confederate monuments across the South, the 2017 white nationalist march through the University of Virginia campus and the murder of a peaceful protestor reopened old wounds. A Democrat was recently, surprisingly, elected to the US Senate from Alabama, and yet the election was won by only a few percentage points. In this election, 68 percent of whites voted Republican and 96 percent of blacks voted Democrat. Southern poets feel these pains and tensions acutely, and many confront them head on in their work. The Henry County, Georgia, of my high school days and the Fulton County of my college days were nothing like Forsyth County (less than an hour north) which, all the way into the late 1980s, terrorized any black person merely passing through. I witnessed very little racism, yet we were racist in many ways, I now realize.

My first poetry teachers were Southerners: Leon Stokesbury and David Bottoms at Georgia State University. Later it was William Logan at the University of Florida, then Austin Hummell, who was from Florida. After receiving my MFA, I followed Hummell to pursue a PhD at the University of North Texas where he, perhaps more than anyone, taught my ear to hear. Bottoms had sung the praises of his Southern heroes, Robert Penn Warren and James Dickey, and Stokesbury had turned me on to Frank Stanford and Miller Williams and more obscure formal writers who seemed completely out of fashion.

Leon Stokesbury put together the last good (to my mind) Southern anthology, *The Made Thing*, published by University of Arkansas Press in 1987, two years after I graduated high school. I was unaware of it till several years later. In 1989, I'd abandoned a study of nuclear engineering at Georgia Tech for a pursuit of poetry at Georgia State. It was a big deal for me to be suddenly in a place where poetry was vibrant and important. Revised for a second edition in 1999, *The Made Thing* has long been the standard of the late twentieth century Southern poem. The poems are mostly free verse, and they are usually established in a clear physical setting and not too experimental, what Stokesbury himself has termed "narrative—almost." Narrative refers to a story that moves through one place and time to another, and many of the poems in his and my anthologies don't do exactly that. They have the trappings of narrative, perhaps the setting and/or the characters, but perhaps not that movement in time—rather a spot in time or what we might call the lyrical moment. Things happen within that one moment, and we might think of this vertically as opposed to being strung along a horizontal timeline. These poems often have some kind of "epiphany" or flash within them that points us to a deeper meaning or set of meanings, often paradoxically. When I have to give an example of paradox, I often think of the physical example of baptism. Yes, the Baptists and immersion. The drowning of the body that results not in death but new life.

Stokesbury's selection was based upon "poets who have published at least one full-length book" and "who were either born and raised in the South or who have lived in the South at least since they began publishing their mature work." That's as good a starting place as any. He also says that his intent "was not to verify any restrictive definition of Southern poetry," although he noticed in the poems he selected "a preoccupation with the past as history" and "a profound relationship to the natural world." These statements seem to me vague and even romantic. How is the past ever not history? Especially if written down. And when has the natural world not been profound? Even *Scientific American* is deep, although it may lack poetry.

My criticism is only of the description of the anthologist's net here and not the contents. Many of the poems in *The Made Thing* helped to shape my aesthetics and poetics, and I am grateful. However, so as to not create overlap, in this anthology I exclude all but one of the poets from the second edition of *The Made Thing*. Alicia Stallings is one of the best poets of my generation (as well, we both are from Georgia, although we never knew each other back then, and we are serious practitioners of traditional forms), so I have included her.

The Made Thing is comparable to the *Morrow Anthology of Younger American Poets* edited by David Bottoms (along with Dave Smith) in 1985. The poems are stylistically similar in their post-Confessional, mostly meditative, image-driven modes. Surely, my own early tastes were formed in the kitchen between these two cookbooks. Most of the poets selected for those two anthologies were teaching in the creative writing programs across the country, and the same is true of this book. One can't really make a living solely as a poet, although certainly poets can do other things besides teach poetry. But it is the vocation that most aptly aligns with the writing of poetry: the sharing it and the studying it. Due to the importance of these two anthologies, my own "past as history" is undeniable in relation to how I see American poetry. Between twelve and my mid-twenties, I grew up in the South. Even though I believe Stokesbury and Bottoms have not received the national recognition they are due (I have to wonder if they have been limited by their very association with Southern poetry, as *merely* Southern poets?), they were two of the primary taste-makers of the late twentieth century. We might look at two of their own best-known poems to see where they're coming from:

Unsent Message to My Brother in His Pain

Please do not die now. Listen.
Yesterday, storm clouds rolled
out of the west like thick muscles.
Lightning bloomed. Such a sideshow
of colors. You should have seen it.
A woman watched with me, then we slept.
Then, when I woke first, I saw
in her face that rest is possible.
The sky, it suddenly seems
important to tell you, the sky
was pink as a shell. Listen
to me. People orbit the moon now.
They must look like flies around
Fatty Arbuckle's head, that new
and that strange. My fellow American,
I bought a French cookbook. In it
are hundreds and hundreds of recipes.
If you come to see me, I shit you not,
we will cook with wine. Listen
to me. Listen to me, my brother,
please don't go. Take a later flight,
a later train. Another look around.

LEON STOKESBURY

Under the Vulture-Tree

We have all seen them circling pastures,
have looked up from the mouth of a barn, a pine clearing,
the fences of our own backyards, and have stood
amazed by the one slow wing beat, the endless dihedral drift.
But I had never seen so many so close, hundreds,
every limb of the dead oak feathered black,

and I cut the engine, let the river grab the jon boat
and pull it toward the tree.
The black leaves shined, the pink fruit blossomed
red, ugly as a human heart.
Then, as I passed under their dream, I saw for the first time
its soft countenance, the raw fleshy jowls
wrinkled and generous, like the faces of the very old
who have grown to empathize with everything.

And I drifted away from them, slow, on the pull of the river,
reluctant, looking back at their roost,
calling them what I'd never called them, what they are,
those dwarfed transfiguring angels,
who flock to the side of the poisoned fox, the mud turtle
crushed on the shoulder of the road,
who pray over the leaf-graves of the anonymous lost,
with mercy enough to consume us all and give us wings.

DAVID BOTTOMS

The themes of death, resurrection, a chance at redemption, and landscape defamiliarized keep me returning to these poems years later. I show them to my students, and they love them. They love the humor of the Stokesbury poem married with the dark sensibility that lies just under the surface—or is it vice versa? And they love the religious connotations of the Bottoms poem pitted against the repugnance of the vultures and their seemingly cursed existence. These strong juxtapositions create imaginative dissonances that result in startling ironies. Surprisingly, there is a kind of hope in many of these poems. It's certainly not true of all Southern poems, but you can see that these verses don't make their dwellings in the darker despairs of the previous generation of Confessional poets.

My teachers, William Logan and Austin Hummell, never expressed to me great interest in geographic or cultural southernness, but they drilled into me the importance of tradition and criticism, of knowing where you came from as a poet and also as a person. And tradition, especially the notion of family (whether genetic or literary), certainly has something to do with the South. Logan grew up in New England and spends half his time now in "Old" England, and Hummell has ended up far north in the Upper Peninsula of Michigan. Are they Southerners? In many ways, they are.

For the purposes of this anthology, I've defined the South as no farther west than Texas, and no farther north than Virginia / DC. But I include even Southern Indiana, because one of the most Southern (and best) poets I've ever had the privilege of working with, Carrie Jerrell, is from there, and she seems more Southern than anybody I know in Florida. Of course, I've included Florida, too, as it is a kind of peculiar South unlike any other. It's important to understand that Jacksonville isn't Tallahassee, and Tallahassee is nothing like Miami or Orlando. The further South you go in Florida, the less Southern it becomes.

Can living in a contemporary city like Atlanta or Tampa, perhaps in a high-rise apartment building, count? Must we write about eating barbecue or speaking in tongues, and will we have some measure of trucks or dogs or whiskey? I go back to what I think Leon Stokesbury told me: family, landscape, religion, and some important tension between comedy and heartbreak. And plainly, we should probably just admit there's something a little bit "country" about the South when we think of it. Something rural—although even that is constantly shifting. The piney woods of Stockbridge, Georgia, where I grew up, hardly exist anymore; the landscape of my youth is now subdivisions as far as the eye can see. Is Stockbridge still the South? It definitely isn't the same South where *I* grew up. Was the South where I grew up even the South? Although then we were surrounded by pine woods, it was still, where I lived, a 1980s typical American subdivision.

Although it is hard to define, there exists this thing we call Southern poetry. Much more so than Midwestern poetry or poetry of the Northwest or California poetry. While the South, itself, might defy definition, poetry is even more seditious. Any poet must admit there is no clear definition of the word "poem." This is because poetry, a rebellious or merely curious child, always challenges its own making, testing its parents (while looking just like them) and striking out for new territory. Poetry's anxiety of influence is unde-niable, and this Freudian complexity is in some ways comforting, in others terrifying. Nevertheless, each poet is blessed or doomed to define a poem—by writing the next poem. Or by compiling the next poetry anthology.

An anthology may pretend to be a house whose inhabitants seem to be familiar, but it is only a door, an entrance to the house of any kind of poetry. I hope that readers might walk through this doorway, make themselves at home, get to know the family, friends, and ghosts herein, and take a look around, or even find some secret passageways to another land altogether. My primary purpose for this anthology is simply to gather together a lot of my favorite poems that happen to be written by Southern poets. Almost arbi-trarily, I have excluded anyone born before 1950. I have tended to include primarily shorter lyric poems because this has been and remains the primary mode of poets in the South. No doubt, in a few years I will have discovered an entirely new collection of fine Southern poems and perhaps feel the need to expand this edition.

A few poets who knew of my plans for this anthology suggested that I lay out the poems thematically, but I found this arrangement would limit the poems in the most obvious ways. And it would skew poems toward singular readings, as if this poem is about race or that one about cooking or Georgia or dysfunctional family. My inten-tional arbitrariness of alphabetical arrangement results in a contigu-ity of poems or poets that might not normally be grouped together, and readers of this book surely would do well to make their own categories of subject matter, themes, tones, forms, styles, etc. that characterize any given set of poems. The way we have it here, if one wants to find a particular poem, it can be accessed quickly.

You will find at the back of this anthology an appendix. The poets were asked to contribute, if they liked, in a paragraph of fewer than 150 words, their answers to the questions "What is Southern poetry?" and/or "What is The South?" I hope the variety of responses satisfy, surprise, and even dissatisfy the reader so that new conversations open, even while simplistic notions of the South fade. This said, I have no doubt that the best poetry of the South is more honest and truthful than any prose statement in getting at this appraisal of Southern identity. It just takes a little more concentration and more time to fathom the depths of the verse. Poetry has a way of getting at the heart of the matter. It tells us who and what we are, and at its best maybe it even points us to who we might become.

JOHN POCH

LUBBOCK, TEXAS, 2020

Gracious

Ablution

Because one must be naked to get clean,
my dad shrugs out of his pajama shirt,
steps from his boxers and into the tub
as I brace him, whose long illness
has made him shed modesty too.

Seated on the plastic bench, he holds
the soap like a caught fish in his lap,
waiting for me to test the water's heat
on my wrist before turning the nozzle
toward his pale skin. He leans over
to be doused, then hands me the soap
so I might scrub his shoulders and neck,
suds sluicing from spine to buttock cleft.

Like a child he wants a washcloth
to cover his eyes while I lather
a palmful of pearlescent shampoo
into his craniotomy-scarred scalp
and then rinse clear whatever soft hair
is left. Our voices echo in the spray
and steam of this room where once,
long ago, he knelt at the tub's edge
to pour cups of bathwater over my head.

He reminds me to wash behind his ears,
and when he judges himself to be clean,
I turn off the tap. He grips the safety bar,
steadies himself, and stands. Turning to me,
his body is dripping and frail and pink.
And although I am nearly forty,
he has this one last thing to teach me.
I hold open the towel to receive him.

AMY FLEURY

3

An Accurate Representation

On our lunch break, we get our passport photos taken
        at the UPS store, and I think I look anxious,
    washed out by the fluorescent lights, but
                    my husband says that's an accurate representation,
reasoning the half frown will make me easy to identify

in any fluorescently lit security line we get stuck in
        on our way to Canada
            on this trip we can't afford, so we pay $11.95
plus tax for each photo, though my mother says
    we can skip the whole thing, if it's too expensive,

                but I suspect she's trying to start something,
    to use me to punish the groom, my brother,
        for his inconvenient destination wedding, the way
children are again and again
                            breaks ~~weapons~~ to be aimed, no matter
their age or their awareness of this, their secondary use.

Regardless, I march my accurate representation of myself
        to the Leon County Clerk of Courts, already
    exasperated, expecting a line, but we walk
                        right up to the counter and the clerk
stamps our forms with no belligerent

                        questioning of our spotty memories
or my lost passport, commenting only
        on my birth date—November 2, 1976, the day
Jimmy Carter was elected—because wouldn't you know it,
                this clerk wrote a book on Jimmy Carter—literally
wrote the book!—which he pulls from behind his high counter
        for me to admire, which I do, delighting him
                with my birth story: how my mother waddled
    to the church hall to cast her ballot for Carter and I slid mewling
        into my place in American history as the votes were tallied,

but when I call my mother to share this serendipitous
          encounter, she protests:
                              She voted for the other guy!
Jimmy Carter was a horrible president! She *never*!
and I realize my willful error of narration: Why would
          my mother, my Republican mother,

                    have voted for Jimmy Carter? Yet I decide on the spot
to keep telling my version—my waddling mother
          casting her democratic ballot in the Baptist church hall
                    before casting her democratic daughter
in the Lee County hospital—in part because I'm fond of

          this history I tailored for myself but also,
                                        I won't deny it,
I thrill childishly at her indignation, and because,
                    since we're being honest, our parents
and our memories, too, become weapons,

                              and here I am practicing my aim.

JOSEPHINE YU

After the Tornado, the Checkout Clerk Considers Leaving

Scene: her apartment

Some states, she knows, are red in fall
and smell like wooded general stores.
Some states are gray all the time, so nothing

newly gray can interrupt their integrity.
Some states wave their flags of birds
and handshakes, some offer peaches on arrival,

some promise eleven feet of snow,
which is a danger you can avoid
by sitting still. Some states are up

where the action is, or at the country's edge
where piers are lit with Ferris wheels
and people still roller skate in short shorts.

Here, today, the sky is blue-dyed, but
the clerk saw the tornado, saw houses
splinter and lift away, as if all along

they had been made of nothing but twine
and toothpicks. Her car is in the driveway, intact.
Her suitcase, her skull, intact. The country

is open and roads are short. She could
be in Arizona by tomorrow. There,
she could watch the sky stay the sky

day after day after day. But some states
dry out your mouth before breakfast. Some states
are a tin drum ringing. Some states outlaw

certain dogs, some promise constant mist,
some grow ice as if it were a crop.
Across town, she knows, are live wires,

rubble, buried limbs. This
is a terrible place now. She watches
her cat continue the work of clawing

the red couch to shreds. The cat doesn't
mind that the couch is an ugly thing,
but then, the cat made it that way.

CATHERINE PIERCE

Allergenesis

They come in their millions, breaking open in the muck. They come with their barnacle bodies blooming. In white, in sulfur colonies they come. Rising from radial engines of dark, from millions of low hatcheries they come, unfolding their jaws sequin by sequin. They come hot & star-limbed & buzzing, with their wire bones, with their names turning edgewise in the mouth. *Bloodweed, Chestbane,* the names. *Knifeclock, Mulehook,* the names. They come lifting themselves long as sentences in air, spiraling down the rifled barrel of the windpipe. Riven & sweltering & swelling, they come into the body's sad lake, its blue bag of steam. So I, Eater of Pith, I Gum Knuckles, I, Threshing Spoon, must move in wiles across the tracheal field, must knock & drag to meet them where they camp, deep in the soft combs of the lungs. Even my breath turns black as I pursue my course. See their millions of insectile wings grown thick with theft. Come, let me clutch at them with my medicine claw & my blood helmet. Down in the fens of histamine.

KIKI PETROSINO

from *Aphorisms*

II.

If you would judge, then be a Judge.

If you would be judged, be just.

The color of a stone is darker in water.

To be loved, love no one.

The catacombs are not the end. Past them lies a wall.

I am an enemy to what I have forgotten.

If a bell rings, then a bell has been moved from its sleep.

Change admits error, but will prove correct in its assumptions.

opposite

Every antipole is itself. Every identity is another.

As I walked along the river, an old man carried a walking stick on his shoulder, as a soldier will carry a rifle. When we passed I greeted him, but he could not bring himself to answer, though I too am an old man, taking pains as I go.

X.

=beauty?

What is the rose but a cup?

Plant seeds in the day's shadows.

Cut pages in their bindings.

Murmurs numb the ears.

If you would be bold, be older.

The alphabet does not spell a word.

AEIOU? I asked in my fever bed.

The heron is not lonely; the loon does not weep.

A friend cannot be lost.

Music to a blind man is Marble.

THEODORE WOROZBYT

4/5/1983

April Fifth, Nineteen Hundred Eighty-Three

Brother came home in flood time, sudden
as the first heave of spring. That week
the river grew restless in its banks, tumbling
out chicken wire and empty bottles in its gorge.
Our house, too, strained, with one more in its tiny rooms:
Father, anxious and crop-hungry, paced the porch
as the waters rose, and Mother at the stove,
her face flushed, weathered our moods in silence.

When the rains broke we worked the bottomland,
Brother sneaking into town at night, proud new muscles
under his thin shirt. One afternoon, the tobacco finally
in the ground, I hid as he met a girl at the end of the road,
imagined words I could not speak—like finding a piano
in the barn, this possibility wide and tense as storm.

DAVIS MCCOMBS

Art in Heaven

wooker

Fishermen lift their question marks from the lake
   in sudden rain. The clean horizon line,
a perfect moon, and its reflection make
     an obelus, a great division sign.
By the shore I walk this glistening road alone—
   singing, against the wind's delirious keening,
     of the glad primal iamb. Divine breath,
   by wizardry of words, gave life to man
to complicate the tale. In the beginning
     was poetry. Then God invented death.

There were shadows, there were shivering and prayer.
   Tatterdemalions crammed inside a cave,
we smelled of our kill and richly of our maker.
     The firelight deemed us lovely, fit to save.
I could reforest Eden with a phrase,
   declare the cursive honeysuckle law,
     he thought, but easy mercy would have marred
   his poem, and he refused to compromise,
too proud to play the *deus ex machina.*
     How can I save my creatures—and my art?

My god, I feel him live—I feel him die.
   Arrows of rain. A lightning claw takes hold
of a leafless tree to shake hands in the sky.
     Some strange white thing, as if the gush of road
were a gentle river, makes the mad descent
   through blue-gray light and crashes, bleeds, transforms.
     Gravity-panicked at the pavement's edge,
   the bird is a book flapping in the wind.
Tomorrow crazed black flies will come in swarms,
     characters loose and hungry for a page.

GREG BROWNDERVILLE

At Lake Mineral Wells State Park

Mineral Wells, Texas, October, 2015

I have brought a group of teenagers
to study their free country. We hike down
a craggy trail, treacherous with boulders
and wild rose vines, just thorns now
this time of year. The oaks are beginning
to turn. I lose my footing,
fall, but in falling find
a rock with moss shaped like a heart.
Blood blooms through my jeans.
I worry about my daughter. I have left
her at school an hour's drive away.
What will happen to her
if something happens to me? I am all
she has for a thousand miles.
The students and I push ourselves
farther than we think we can go.
Out of dense forest the deep blue lake
opens ahead of us, and we pause.
Leaf shadows vibrate on the humus.
A woodpecker rattles its brain for a taste.
We keep going. My heart limps inside me.
A lizard hurries across my line of sight.
I think of home. The usual pain
of being far from it is lessened here.
Through branches, the sun shows lines
of monofilament. Mid-air, a spider,
small and gray as lint, throws balls
of silk to the wind, hoping they catch
and take hold.

DANIELLE SELLERS

The Avocado

"In 1971, drunk on the sweet, sweet juice of revolution,
a crew of us marched into the president's office with a list
of demands," the black man tells us at the February luncheon,
and I'm pretending I haven't heard this one before as I eye
black tortillas on a red plate beside a big green bowl
of guacamole made from the whipped, battered remains
of several harmless former avocados. If abolitionists had a flag
it would no doubt feature the avocado, also known as the alligator
pear, for obvious reasons. "Number one: reparations!
Enough gold to fill each of our women's wombs, gold
to nurse our warriors waiting to enter this world with bright fists,
that's what we told them," the man says, and I'm thinking
of the money-colored flesh of the avocado, high in monosaturates;
its oil content is second only to olives. I am looking
at Yoyo's caterpillar locks dangle over her ear. I dare you
to find a lovelier black woman from Cincinnati, where the North
touches the South. "Three: we wanted more boulevards
named for the Reverend Dr. Martin Luther King Jr. An airport
named for Sojourner Truth." The roots of the avocado tree
can raise pavement, so it's not too crazy to imagine the fruit
as a symbol of revolt on the abolitionist flag. We are all one kind
of abolitionist or another, no doubt. And we are like the avocado
    too
with its inedible ruby-colored seed that can actually sprout from
    inside
when the fruit is overmature, causing internal molds and
    breakdown.
"Demand number twenty-one: a Harriet Tubman statue on the
    mall!"
Brother man is weeping now and walking wet tissue to the trash
    can
and saying, "Harriet Tubman was a walking shadow," or, "Harriet
    Tubman
walked in shadows," or "To many, Harriet Tubman was a shadow
to walk in," and the meaning is pureed flesh with lime juice,

14

minced garlic, and chili powder; it is salt, and the pepper
Harriet Tubman tossed over her shoulder to trouble the
     bloodhounds.
Many isolated avocado trees fail to fruit from lack of pollination.
"Goddamn, ain't you hungry?" I whisper to Yoyo, and she puts a
     finger
to my lips to distract me. Say, baby, wasn't that you waking me up
last night to say you'd had a dream where I was a big luscious
     mansize
avocado? Someone's belly is growling. "We weren't going
to be colored, we weren't going to be Negro," the man says,
and I'm thinking every time I hear this story it's the one telling the
     story
that's the hero. "Hush now," Harriet Tubman probably said
near dawn, pointing a finger black enough to be her pistol barrel
toward the future or pointing a pistol barrel black enough
to be her finger at the mouth of some starved, stammering slave
and then lifting her head to listen for something no one but her
     could hear.

TERRANCE HAYES

Balloon Heart

For days after the wedding,
she left the balloon heart
hanging on her car's antenna.
She liked the way the limp
bubble drooped and bounced
each day becoming emptier,
heavier, less like a celebration.
After three weeks it snowed.
By then the heart had slid down
until it touched the hood,
and as she drove, the thing,
now frozen, knocked and knocked
like knuckles on a hard wood desk,
like an ice pick chipping away.

BETH GYLYS

Banking Hours

Time to get down to business. Time to settle
accounts and round the sums.
The sun's loose change lies scattered on the floor
and shade has inched between the pansies and the mums.
The piper's all played out, the whore's been diddled,
and the shops have closed their doors.

Time to square with the clock's big jaundiced eye
as it glares back at you;
with those two sweeping hands that meet like shears
when you wake up not sure yet if the dream was true.
Time to answer the phone and tell us why
your payments are in arrears.

Time to admit the check was never "in
the mail," that you were never
"between jobs currently," nor was your card
mischarged, stolen, lost. You've always been so clever.
You've always had a tendency to spend
more than you could afford.

How easily you fall for cheap distractions:
long nights, gossip and girls,
the highball tumbler sweating along its facets.
How easily, old swine, you fritter away your pearls
for one more chance to nose the world's confections,
squandering your assets

until, look, it's late; the leaves have gone the way
of dames and dollars now.
The spider's tallied up her last gauze beads
on the web strung between the porch and locust bough.
That wind sounds like the rake of a croupier
combing the yellow weeds.

So run the spreadsheets. Balance the register.
You knew, of course—didn't you?—
the bill would post, that notice for both prime
and principal: Records Show. Please Pay Amount Due.
It's time to make good with your creditor.
Soon ends will meet. It's time,

dear customer, it's time.

MORRI CREECH

Bardo

Yeah, I'm having to watch that right now,
my brother said, "That," being the slow death of our dad,
Spike.

My brother was at the pool talking to a woman
with a prison tat, her boobs somehow
up and full as two oranges.
Bikini tops are amazing things, he thought,
not fully understanding the simplicity of synthetics.

        What she said next, the woman sunbathing
        with the tits and prison tat,
was that traditional Japanese Buddhists believe
no one is fully alive until the 7th birthday.
    Life something you become filled with—
    like water pouring from a pitcher into the body.

Dying takes a long time, too, he said, thinking about
Spike pissing himself by the packaged Swiss
and shredded Mozzarella in the Kroger aisle.
That darkness spreading across the crotch of his tan pants
      and moving down his right leg in a wobbly line
      like water pouring from a pitcher.
The look in his eyes: scared, apologetic.
And then he blinked. Smiled.
      Began humming "In the Mood—"
      a song he'd danced to with all the girls in the fifties.
      He was no longer there, no longer in Kroger,
      when he stepped forward and reached out both arms
      toward the brightly lit rows of cheese,
      all the while humming, *Don't keep me waiting,*
      don't keep me waiting,
      when I'm in the mood.

CHARLOTTE PENCE

Beer

A mildly alcoholic beverage
Made from a malted, farinaceous grain
Combined with choice hops and allowed to age,
Beer's "proof God loves us" (Franklin), and we'd fain

Have beer, beer's having given us so much,
Beer bong, beer gut and goggles, beer-induced
Liaisons, bless its beery heart—a crutch?
No way, man, (beer me) you are getting *juiced*—

Until you split to meet the great Beer Man,
Himself, it's Party Time (they serve
An ice cold draft) and you're a legend here,
Immortalized in stone, an artisan,
Artiste—the grit, the showmanship, the verve,
And your last words, "Watch this, man.
                                    Hold my beer."

GREG WILLIAMSON

Believer

I hadn't wanted to believe myself
numbered among the unlucky ones.
There'd always seemed an arrogance in that
of which my superstition made me wary.
Nor was the title very accurate.
In fact it seemed a blessing or a talent
sometimes, or its own kind of deeper luck,
the way I walked into each suffering
which was its own intricate world complete
with wild children wrangling to be king
of every broken square of concrete
and market stalls of shrimp kept cool on ice
whose infinitesimal limbs caught light
as if hauled glittering into genesis.

DANIELLE CHAPMAN

Bellocq's Ophelia

from a photograph, circa 1912

In Millais's painting, Ophelia dies faceup,
eyes and mouth open as if caught in the gasp
of her last word or breath, flowers and reeds
growing out of the pond, floating on the surface
around her. The young woman who posed
lay in a bath for hours, shivering,
catching cold, perhaps imagining fish
tangling in her hair or nibbling a dark mole
raised upon her white skin. Ophelia's final gaze
aims skyward, her palms curling open
as if she's just said, *Take me.*

I think of her when I see Bellocq's photograph —
a woman posed on a wicker divan, her hair
spilling over. Around her, flowers —
on a pillow, on a thick carpet. Even
the ravages of this old photograph
bloom like water lilies across her thigh.
How long did she hold there, this other
Ophelia, nameless inmate in Storyville,
naked, her nipples offered up hard with cold?

The small mound of her belly, the pale hair
of her pubis — these things — her body
there for the taking. But in her face, a dare.
Staring into the camera, she seems to pull
all movement from her slender limbs
and hold it in her heavy-lidded eyes.
Her body limp as dead Ophelia's,
her lips poised to open, to speak.

NATASHA TRETHEWEY

Bite Me

You who are all clichés of babysoft
crawl to my rocking chair,
pull up on my knees,
lift your delicate finger to the silver balloon
from your first birthday,
open your warm red mouth
and let float your word, your fourth
in this world, *Bawoooooon*—
then, delighted, bite my thigh.
I practice my stern *No*. You smile,
then bite my shin. *No*, I say again,
which feels like telling the wind *No*
when it blows. But how to stop you?
This month you've left your mark on me
through sweatshirts and through jeans,
six-teeth-brooches that take a week to fade
from my collarbone, hip, wrist.
What fierceness in that tiny
snapping jaw, your after-grin.
You don't bite your teething rings,
don't bite your toys, your crib,
other children, or your father.
It makes us wonder.

                    Daughter,
when you were nearly here,
when you were crowning
and your father could see your black hair
and lifted in his trembling hands
the scissors to cut your tie to me,
when a nurse had gone to the waiting room
to assure my mother *Just a few more pushes*,
when another had the heat lamp
warming the bassinet beside my cot,
then held up the mirror so I could see you sliding out—

you started turning. Wriggling
your elbows up. The mandala
of your black hair turning and turning
like a pinwheel, like laundry in the eye
of the washer, like the eye of the storm
that was just beginning
and would finish me off, forever,
because you did it,
you got stuck, quite stuck,
and so, they said, I'd have to push
head-shoulders-elbows out at once.

                            And Lord
did I push, for three more hours
I pushed, I pushed so hard I shat,
pushed so hard blood vessels burst
in my neck and in my chest, pushed so hard
my asshole turned inside-out like a rosebud,
pushed so hard that for weeks to come
the whites of my eyes were red with blood,
my face a boxer's, swollen and bruised,
though I wasn't thinking then
about the weeks to come
or anything at all besides pushing and dying,
and your father was terror and blood splatter
like he too was being born
and he was, we were,
and finally I burst at the seams
and you were out,
Look, Ha, you didn't kill me after all,
Monster I have you,
and you are mine now, mine,

and it is no great wonder
that you bite me—
because you were crowning
and had to eat your way out of me,
because you were crowning

and developed a taste
for my royal blood.

BETH ANN FENNELLY

Blues for the Death of the Sun

The evening sun descended with the decorum of an old man
Who removes his wide-brimmed hat as a funeral march passes.
August. The rivers rose. We saw the sun vanish.
Like crows, the people of my town pace the streets, faces skyward.
From wet ground ferns spring, fronds greening with hunger.
The river reeks of gasoline burning in her current.
Across the blackened hills I hear a peacock holler his blue yodel.
Your hands ain't wings, a passing stranger tells me.
The sky has taken away light.
Is it punishment? the newspapers ask. *We thought God was dead.*
The newspaper printed this as if God could read.
I stand here waiting for something to happen.
An empty glass soda bottle rolls down the road.
The live oak's leaves seem to fatten with every passing minute.
I watched as the people of my town tore down a man
With their bare hands. They say he stole the light with his curse,
But I only thought he was talking to himself.
I ask the sky, *How come your hands left us?*
How does the ocean feel about no light? How quiet is her bell.
My people in the streets, calling. Their drowned faces.
A people, a piano, can't live without light.
People say that even if we go to the top of the mountain,
Even then we can't reach the light.
Our sky, bereft. Our heartmuscle, lit into blue flame.
We gnaw for light that lies beneath our skin.
We've turned to flames
Like a house burning itself from the inside out.

ANSEL ELKINS

Boy

Boy, let me have a taste of that Mister Misty.
No, they brought it out around the time you
were born in sixty. I like the way it swish
in the cup. Sound like Sammy Davis Jr.
doing the soft shoe shuffle. They call
that the sand dance. Sound like shifting grains
or a fast train. Them little bits of ice
tap your teeth, and you can chew on that sweet
mouthful of cold melting to nothing before
you swallow it down. First time I had one
of these, I drank it too fast, crystals in syrup
dancing around and down my throat chilled
like Christmas and New Year's cold breath moving
down to my chest. And if that wasn't enough,
then I felt like my head was about to split
right open. Thought my forehead was gon look
like that Dairy Queen sign red and wide
like a gash. You know, they ice cream got nothing
on your mama's pineapple ice cream. Theirs
ain't nothing but soft light ice milk. They build
it high like a steeple, but ain't nothing
to that either. You see your mama puts
a dozen eggs in her custard to make
it rich. The sound of the ice and salt shifting
in that bucket as it melts with that electric
churn's whining motor groaning as that ice
cream stiffens up sure is pleasing cause I know
the ice cream about ready. You know, there are
folks getting they heads split so we don't have
to go around to that side window no more.

SEAN HILL

Burying Albatross

In the parking lot behind the funeral home, my eyes settle on
the bulky white noose my father has lost a wrestling match to.
Though he is not convinced Windsor knot know-how can plant
tobacco or drive a nail true, he concedes his flawed results,

abides my desire to fix it. Calling up knowledge passed to me
from a book, I execute the maneuvers with fluid precision
and imagine I am creasing and folding a Japanese paper swan.
He stares at my knuckles, smiling, perhaps seeing his own hands

stuccoing a high ceiling or replacing a worn-out alternator.
Standing close enough to kiss, we almost touch and pretend
to bury other heavy things, sewn together like the opposite ends
of the fabric in my hands. Before I let him go, all the sage advice

and words of encouragement that never breathed air between us
spread a silent wing then slide through a perfect slip knot, home.

FRANK X. WALKER

Butt-Naked Old Men

Not a pretty picture
in the public pool locker room,
but now, now, no need to get all
ubi sunt or *carpe diem* about it.

So once upon a time that slackened anatomy
embodied Adonis in somebody's eyes,
the incarnation of a trembling crush
exquisitely fulfilled or forever unrequited,

and now stands crushed itself,
skin discolored, whatever the color,
and overgrown with growths enough
to keep dermatologists dancing.

As for that distinguishing feature
among these noontime nudists, the one that meant
frustration to some, triumph to others,
and to a few a bothersome distraction,

it looks unlikely its status will be
ever elevated to most preferred.

But stick that pity in some other ear;

once upon a time can only deject
those who live so far beyond it,

unlike a new mother just diagnosed
and never to bare her fatal breasts,
lucky to last and wither at last,

over on the ladies' side.

STEPHEN CUSHMAN

Bycatch

Not the almighty succulent shrimp
hand-picked like jewels from the pile
hauled in and dumped by the trawl,

nor even the clichéd rubber boot,
nor the terrified and pathetic dolphin.
Not Ophelia in her muddy dress,

her mouth forever opened in song,
yet still it meant money: *square grouper*,
the deck crew coined their bycatch

when they withdrew from the ocean
two fifty-five-gallon drums of cocaine.
But even then no long moral debate,

nor any predicament about what to do.
This was it: an exit from the stench-work
of fish guts and salt-covered waders,

seagulls forever screaming behind them
like a requiem for lives of prosperity.
So the crew sold it all summer and waded

in the money. *We know what we are but
know not what we be*, Ophelia mumbled
before her leap into the river, and who

among them thought they'd be caught
like shrimp or dolphin or rubber boots
in the profiteering nets of the law?

HASTINGS HENSEL

Cedar Key after Storm

The fish shacks turned an oystery glow,
the drowned light more intense.
Along the blank sky low
clouds learned from experience.

A bridge leapt over the inlet
where sawtooth reeds had bedded,
like spears in rusting silhouette,
as the summer storm receded.

Carved from gray blocks of wood,
enormous sad pelicans
on the concrete balustrade stood
stiff as librarians,

as if they dimly knew
the mighty events to come.
The distant thunder grew
fainter, like a brushed kettle-drum.

And you were a great bird, sickly,
fleeing the northern weather.
Ten years had passed quickly
since we watched the Gulf together.

Look back now at the theft
of boredom, and jazz, and the rages,
and see what little is left—
just a book of the thinnest pages.

Your voice was the gentlest whisper,
your health had gone so fast.
Of all the things you were,
perhaps that would be the last.

i.m. Donald Justice (1925–2004)

WILLIAM LOGAN

Coat Hanger Bent Into Halo

Gathering up my mother's clothes for the poor,
I find the coat hanger that almost aborted me,
or so I dub it—the last hand clung to the high rod.
       Unwould, it could have poked

through the pink, puckered hold of her cervix
to spill me before I got going good.
Instead, from the furred litter of souls squirming
       to be visible, I was picked.

May I someday spy Mother's poppy-studded hat
on the skull of a street-corner gospel singer
swarming with sores. May I twist from this black wire
       a halo to crown my son's head.

MARY KARR

Concerning My Former In-Laws

I'd been promised my one and only
white Christmas

as we gathered around their usual
poinsettias in lieu of a tree

I just couldn't tamp myself down
I didn't know what was going to happen

I kept fogging the storm door
where the heat was leaving

yes many are passionate for snow
you can always find yourself another

my in-laws seemed to be charmed
by my particular hope

I wasn't yet gone from them
the next stop that night was my mother's

the road still clear   it hadn't yet started
I saw a ring around the moon

yes I believed
later that they would call

if only to ask me if I had what I needed
outside looking up

and up into a sky
that was falling   my face

meeting again and again
such cold

JULIE FUNDERBURK

The Confession

I could draw you a picture if I had a mind to.
Out past the last road there were woods and a still.

There were cars in front of a ramshackle barn,
The moon in a cloud and a tree on the hill.

I remember the raw December weather,
Boys shouting curses and most of them drunk.

I remember the wind in the barley stubble.
I remember the man they dragged from the trunk.

The moon appeared and disappeared.
Headlights and whiskey. A tree on the hill.

We tied the knot and we threw it over.
It took half an hour for his legs to go still.

Just boys, for all that, in December weather,
Settling a grievance, correcting a wrong.

I remember one shoe kicked off in the heather.
I remember my feet hurt from standing so long.

The place may be there. I could draw you a picture.
The moon in a cloud and a tree on the hill.

Damned if I know how I see it so clearly.
Don't ask me to speak of it. Damned if I will.

MORRI CREECH

Conversation with Owl and Clouds

Owl-night, moon-gone, my wherewithal
is yellow pine. Is trillium and unfurled frond.

Clouds,—a cantilever of the trees, vapor-
plied architecture of the ephemeral—teach me

the apparition-life, what tunes the branches'
nocturne off-key: how do bodies turn into

song? Glow of dust and sandstone light, stars
dropped like pebbles, like crumbs, heretofore

a fairy tale trail. Barn owl, secretive and out-
spoken, you spout two minds, a hiding place

and a traffic sign. What's this absence
you speak of? Nonsense-yakking *lost soul,*

lost soul, the self-question that grows—
Who what?—odd and old.

Build me up into the fog, into brevity
made beautiful, the wet-dressed disaster

that's rain, that's the storm-threat of forest fire.
I want to be ornate and ornery. More than

a vapor-child, a night's ward like the white
monkshood tucking under its bud, too shameful

to flower. I am hearing it: spring's first wild melt,
each drop trickling into the next, a minor

chord. So snow's gone, so how can I be
ice dissolving in water?

Cloud me, sparrowing and bark-loose,
each season's dark ambition: a patient pattern

gone. O, I am hearing it: this say-nothing
noise, how the world's clamor-born and

sorrowful, tricked for loss, the silent purpling
of crocuses mouthing back at the owl:

I will not, and soon—

JENNIFER CHANG

Cosmogony

A ball of yarn, a hill
maintain an equipoise until
          their neatness starts to bore the gods
             of potential and energy
         who hedge bets, reckoning the odds
           of when the rest will be

set in motion, and who,
first stumbling upon this clew,
          constructed both the incline and
             the inclination to unwind.
         Like most gods, though, they haven't planned
           to stay; they mastermind

the scheme, *ex nihilo,*
then slip behind the shadow show
         and designate an agent, chief
             remaker of their mischief made.
        Each time, disguised, this leitmotif
          gets salvaged and replayed,

a universe begins,
for orogens and origins
         suppose a Way Things Were before
             some volatile, untimely That—
        sweetness perverted by the core
         or the belfry by the bat,

or here, a hilly green,
whose still life, eerily serene,
         completes their best contrivance yet:
             from high above, a williwaw,
        a hiss, and then the silhouette
          of one terrific paw.

CAKI WILKINSON

Country-Western Singer

I used to feel like a new man A
After the day's first brew. B
But then the new man I became A
Would need a tall one too. B

As would the new man he became, A
And the new one after him, B
And so on and so forth till the new men made A
The dizzy room go dim. B

And each one said, I'll be your muse, A
I'll trade you song for beer. B
He said, I'll be your salt lick, honey, C
If you will be my deer. B

He said, I'll be your happy hour, A
And you, boy, you'll be mine. B
And mine won't end at six or seven C
Or even at closing time. B

Yes, son, I'll be your spirit guide, A
I'll lead you to Absolut, B
To Dewar's, Bushmills, and Jameson C
Then down to Old Tanglefoot. B

And there I'll drain the pretense from you A
That propped you up so high; B
I'll teach you how salvation's just C
Salivation without the I. B

To hear his sweet talk was to think A
You'd gone from rags to riches, B
Till going from drink to drink became C
Like going from hags to bitches, B

A
B   or   A
A   B
B   C
         B

Like going from bed to barroom stool, **A**
From stool to bathroom stall, **B**
From stall to sink, from sink to stool, **A**
From stool to hospital. **B**

The monitors beep like pinball machines, **A**
And coldly the IV drips, **B**
And a nurse runs a moistened washcloth over **C**
My parched and bleeding lips. **B**

And the blood I taste, the blood I swallow **A**
Is as far away from wine **B**
As 5:10 is for the one who dies **C**
at 5:09. **B**

ALAN SHAPIRO

The Country-Western Singer's Ex-Wife, Sober in Mendocino County, California

Somewhere back East my late love's all coked up,
another cowgirl wannabe lying
at his feet while he plucks a Willie Nelson song
from his beer-soaked six string and complains nobody
understands a rebel's broken heart.
I've played her part, the starstruck blonde in boots

and denim mini, boobs and brains to boot.
Whiskey-fed, dreamy, how I talked him up,
a sequined Tammy to his George, my heart
a backstage bed I wanted him to lie in.
It proved too hard, and when a harder body
came along, he said, *The party's over*,

and left me listening to "Sad Songs and Waltzes,"
Waylon, steel guitars that struck like a boot
to the face. But that's good country, right? A body
enamored with its bruises, praising its screw-ups,
the blood still wet in its wounds? Memory lies
as still as a rattlesnake until my heart

begs for its venom. *Sink 'em in*, my heart
says. *I've been traveling on a horse called Music,
and he's brought me here to die.* I'd be lying
if I said I didn't want to fill my ex's boots
with spit the night I caught him with that up-
start starlet at the bar; when everybody

tried to hide in their shot glasses; when nobody
but a Broadway street preacher had the heart
to hold my hair off my face while I threw up
outside; when all the songs I loved—"Crazy,"

"Golden Ring," "Jolene"—became like boots
too busted to put on, bent-pitch ballads of his lies,

my shame sung loud in the key of C. He's lying
from the stage, in the bar or bed, when he says nobody
understands him. I do. I've burned my boots,
moved west to wine and water because his heart
was a dry bottle, cold as the black rose
rotting in his lapel, and I still wake up

to his tunes: the beer, blow, boots and love, the lies
they tell and don't. Once, I was a good-hearted woman.
Now I pray, Lord, please, somebody, shut him up.

CARRIE JERRELL

Death by Basketball

Before and after school
he stood
on a milk crate
eyeballed the mirror
and only saw wayne turner
an all-american
at tournament time

a third grader
just off the bus
barely four feet
off the ground
he dropped his books
sank a j'
from the top of the key
and heard the crowd roar
beat his man off the dribble
with a break yaneck
crossover
and slammed himself
on the cover of a box
of wheaties

he was out there
every night
under a street light
fighting through double picks
talking trash
to imaginary body checks
'you can't hold me fool'
fake right
'this is my planet'
drive left
'is the camera on'
reverse lay-up

'that's butter baby'
finishing with a trey
from downtown, swish!
'I'm inna zone t'night
whogotnext?'

more than a little
light in the ass
hands so small
the ball almost dribbled him
he formed his own lay-up line
in the bluegrass
wildcat jersey
hanging like a summer dress
on a court made bald
from daily use
and instead of writing
his spelling words
he signed a contract
he could barely read
inked a commitment
in big block letters
to the NBA
and NIKE
and SPRITE
scribbled superstar in cursive
with a fat red pencil
and practiced his
million dollar smile
not his multiplication table
thinking of how many
chocolate milks
he could buy
with his signing bonus
or his all-star game
appearance fee
after recess

another shooting
another tragic death
another little genius
who will never test out
of a dream
that kills legitimate futures
every night
under street lights
wherever these products
are sold

FRANK X. WALKER

The Dive

A busted exit sign above the door
invites no one to leave. The windows are barred,
and the panes themselves are painted over with tar.
No question as to what this place is for.

The regulars all stare into their drinks,
lamenting futures, forgetting pasts. Bar stools
are split at every seam. The TAVERN RULES
say No Cussing, though mostly no one speaks.

They're married to their grief, you think. But here
you are: Jack Daniel's and your worries. The same
as any drunk who will not lay the blame
on himself, drowning instead in whisky and beer.

A man with roadmap eyes searches his pockets
for jukebox change and comes up short. Instead,
the ceiling fan keeps rhythm while each dead
minute tumbles off the High Life clock. "It's

closing time!" Time for another drink.
The barkeep brings it over, snatches the cash,
flicks his cigarette and drops the ash
into the rusted pit of a clogged-up sink.

This dive, this glass, these greasy fingerprints,
they're each a part of something very old:
a need to slow the way a story's told
to keep it all from making too much sense.

CHAD ABUSHANAB

Dream Transient

After reading Bolaño

I'm in one of Borges' dreams. He chases me like a dog. I try to dream of the word *labyrinth*. Borges doesn't let me. He tells me it's impossible to give it shape. In his dream I'm not allowed to dream. He said.

I dream I see through my grandfather's eyes. I see a man folding dollar bills into his wallet. I see a paper gun. I see the shawl of a woman, and a woman without a shawl. I see grief as a spider. I see bottles of beer. I see a man falling off a horse. I see a cactus. I see. He was blind.

My daughter tells me she had a dream about me. I sketched a house made of cardboard. Then I preached inside the house. Then there was a mob. Someone ran me out of town. I found a river. I crossed the river. I found a woman. The woman was her mother. I loved her mother. Then I woke up. I told my daughter I had a dream about her.

I dream my ex-lover dreams about me. We hold hands. We kiss. We have a black child. He calls me by another man's name. His mother tells me I'm worthless. She makes the child disappear. We're alone. My hands and feet are tied. She whips me with the wet backbone of adultery. I try to remember her name so she may stop. Andrea. Samantha. Mercy.

OCTAVIO QUINTANILLA

Dust Devil

Mystical hysterical amalgam of earth and wind
and mind

over and of
the much-loved

dust you go
through a field I know

by broken heart
for I have learned this art

of flourishing
vanishing

wherein to live
is to move

cohesion
illusion

wild untouchable toy
called by a boy

God's top
in a time when time stopped

CHRISTIAN WIMAN

Early Autumn in Tennessee

Before October's gold veneer
Of leaf has covered the chilled creek,
And all the trees have grown antique
With change, before the wind unveils
Each rickety and grim physique
Of maple, poplar, oak, and elm,
The cotton downs the drying field
Like strange, anachronistic snow.
The monarchs come. The monarchs go.
But still there are late swallowtails,
The cloudless sulfurs, too, that glow
Like incandescent lemon skins.
Just yesterday the evening sky
Grew gas-blue like a pilot light.
The meadow purpled into night.
And as a flock of grackles came
The black confetti of their flight
Seemed suddenly to shape a slurred,
Profoundly large and fleeting word
Against the cool and fragile dusk.
At the meadow's far end I heard
The downward spiraling of song.
It was a screech owl's shrill reply
To what was written on the clear sky,
Though, really, who could comprehend
The meaning of that mournful cry?
The air was sweet with soil and hay.
Two jet trails hooked a loose crochet
Across the writhing apple-green
And phlox-blue of the dying day.
It was a feeling more than a thought
That those cold colors smoldering there
Seemed like the colors despair
Or some unnamable regret.
While such forebodings, it is true,

Will seldom sway the courts of law,
Or topple legislative chambers,
They may give prophets pause, or make
The broken-hearted exiles weep,
And this, for many, is enough.

DANIEL ANDERSON

Election Day Shooting at Middleburg, Tennessee, November 4, 1924, With Excerpts from the November 7 Edition of *The Lexington Progress* and Auburn Powers's *History of Henderson County*

Hattie Lloyd Todd, aged eleven, saw them fall in the street—Tuke
      Bartholomew and his son Bud, the Democrats in charge
of the ballot box. In a few years she would be married to the
      nephew of the next man to die. He was W. W. Rogers, a
      Republican
and son of Tennessee Unionists, shot through the head when he
      tried to talk some sense to his friend Dan Powers,
who was wielding the gun that day of the national election and a
      fair marksman even when blind with rage. The assassin
      walked away

unpursued. Everyone in three counties traveled to Oak Grove
      Cemetery in such conveyances as were available, three
      fresh graves
spaded out of the clay, a year's worth of funerals on a single
      afternoon. Dan Powers hid out in the barns and corncribs
      of sympathizers
until he fled in the night, months of vagabondage taking him as
      far as Mexico and then Cuba before returning home to
      face a jury
of neighbors and distant kin. Not long into his life sentence, he
      took a razor to his throat, this killer of three people, one
      of them

his own good friend. There's not much burg to Middleburg
          anymore. The store burned down; the farms were
          foreclosed on. No call
to go back except to bury the dead. At the end of a long and
          fretful life Hattie Lloyd Todd was laid to rest while a blue
          jay scolded
from the lower limbs of a cemetery oak. We always considered my
          grandmother to be as flighty as a songbird, touched by
          fears
and superstitions, and wouldn't have thought to ask what went
          through her head every time an engine backfired.
          Any dark cloud

reminded her of the tornado that spun their house down a hill
          and left it next to a splintered Spanish oak. I recalled
          asking her,
"Where'd you go?" She was defenseless against the memory. "We
          tacked up a little more tar paper," she said, "and went on
          living in it."

BOBBY ROGERS

52

English Sonnet

London returns in damp, fragmented flurries
when I should be doing something else. A scrap
of song, a pink scarf, and I'm back to curries
and pub food, long, wet walks without a map,
bouts of bronchitis, a case of the flu,
my half-hearted studies, and brooding thoughts
and scanning faces in every bar for you.
Those months come down to moments or small plots,
like the bum on the Tube, enraged that no one spoke,
who raved and spat, the whole car thick with dread,
only to ask, won't someone tell a joke?
and this mouse of a woman offered, *What's big and red
and sits in the corner?*
                              A naughty bus.
Not funny, I know. But neither's the story of us.

CHELSEA RATHBURN

Exercitia Spiritualia

We met, like lovers in movies, on a quay
Beside the Seine. I was reading Foucault
And feeling smart. She called him *an assault
On sense,* and smiled. She was from Paraguay,

Was reading Saint Ignatius. Naivete
Aroused her, so she guided me to Chartres
And Sacré-Coeur, to obscure theatres
For passion plays—she was my exegete.

In Rome (for Paris hadn't been enough)
We took a room, made love on the worn parquet,
Then strolled to Sant'Ignazio. Strange duet:
Pilgrim and pagan, gazing, as though through

That ceiling's flatness, toward some epitome
Of hoped-for depth. I swore I saw a dome.

GEOFFREY BROCK

Explaining an Affinity for Bats

That they are only glimpsed in silhouette,
And seem something else at first—a swallow—
And move like new tunes, difficult to follow,
Staggering towards an obstacle they yet
Avoid in a last-minute pirouette,
Somehow telling solid things from hollow,
Sounding out how high a space, or shallow,
Revising into deepening violet.

That they sing—not the way the songbird sings
(Whose song is rote, to ornament, finesse)—
But travel by a sort of song that rings
True not in utterance, but harkenings,
Who find their way by calling into darkness
To hear their voice bounce off the shape of things.

A. E. STALLINGS

explosives

a	bomb	is a	statement	a	poem	is a	question
a	bomb	is what a	state meant	a	poem	is a	quest
the pleasure		of your	mental	a	poem		requests
		your	state mentality	energy			
a	bomb		state	is a	poem	isn't it	request
		makes a	state(ment)	makes		a	
	bomb	the sent i	meant			of the	
		is	(st)ate	you ear			
				you heard		the	question
drop a	bomb	on em					
			state	your			request
stop the	bombing						question
the		your	state			you can't	question
			state	in			
		your	state	of disarray			
		what a	state	we're in a	poem	we	request
a	bomb shelter	from the	statement	storm		a	sequester

she's a	bombshell	in a	state	of	po(em)	ver(i)ty	
		your	state	of mind		your	question
stop	bombing	your closing	statement	please repeat		your	request
da	bomb			dis	poem	is	
to blow up				dis	poem	is about	

EVIE SHOCKLEY

Exteriority

Maybe I'm not very human—
what I wanted to do was to paint
sunlight on the side of a house.

—Edward Hopper

The barn: a Rembrandt inside,
its air mahogany; dust-choked,
hay-flown; reeking of manure,
dried blood, a rich, animal must.

But here, in its dense shade, bales
unloaded and stacked, the old truck
waiting while we smoke, crouched,
with sweat-soaked, crooked backs

propped against the cool tin, we see,
gazing across the yard to the small
wood-frame farmhouse, how sunlight
blazes on its white clapboard walls,

stokes it like a bellows, makes it
bloom, and how a mockingbird clings
to the peak of its gable, light,
like light, borne, as it is, on wings.

NICK NORWOOD

Faith

Picture a city
and the survivors: from their
windows, some scream. Others
walk the aftermath: blood
and still more blood coming
from the mouth of a girl.

This is the same movie
playing all over
the world: starring everybody
who ends up where the action
is: lights, cameras, close-ups—*that*
used to be somebody's leg.

Let's stop talking
about *God*. Try to shut-up
about heaven: some of our friends
who should be alive   are no longer alive.
Moment by moment death moves
and memory doesn't remember,

not for long: even today—even
having said
this, even knowing that
someone is stealing
our lives—I still
had lunch.

Tell the truth. If you can.
Does it matter   who they were,
the bodies in the rubble: could it matter

that the girl was conceived by two people
buried in each other's arms, believing
completely in the world between them?

The commanders are ready. The guns
walk everywhere. Almost all of them
believe in God. But somebody should

hold a note   for the Earth,
a few words for whatever being

human   could mean
beneath the forgotten sky:

some day one night,
when the city lights go out for good,

you won't believe how many stars

TIM SEIBLES

Fake Flowers

I was walking along my normal route, dog
loose on her long lead like a kite led
by the breeze of her sensing snout, O'Hara
talking about wristwatches and cats
playing in sawdust, and you
back in our apartment, still naked,
unsure you'll shower off the sweat
or just go to work glazed by it. There
are flowers tossed down a hillside of dead leaves,
plastic purple with white centers, my eye
went straight to them. The crows
gathered around inexplicable leftovers,
alerted by a scout: rising up in reverse confetti.
A dog barking somewhere in a barrel.
All of this now in my head—converging
streets at Times Square, castoff photos
from *The Americans*, miscropped, blurry.
The way you pad around the place, topless,
reading the *Times*, playing a scratchy
Wardell Gray album, makes me
want to bring you back this gift.

SEBASTIAN MATTHEWS

Ferocious Ode

It tells you the name of the flower you love.
It takes the shape of an old woman working
a pitchfork in the hay of a garden growing
voluptuously every day in your heart, that is

to say *it*, being mysterious, is difficult to
describe simply and with candor. It grabs
children in their dreams like tigers grab
gazelles. It grabs tigers. It makes me say

the sweet convolutions of poetry are not so
sweet sometimes and my grandfather claws
the red clay walls of hell for what he did to
my father. And I am happy on summer days

when the lily that I love bobs and sways
in wind like fire on a ladder. It matters.
Like a ladder on fire, it is spiritual. Like
the simile in which a house burns down

inside a boy, it is tragic. It turns and turns
laughing like a nun. It is nonsequential,
baffling and close to death like a woman
turning a pitchfork in her garden. Her diary

reads "I loved him." It is one page after
the last page in my grandmother's diary.
It is afternoon and the sun is setting
coldly over my father's head—the oval

of which he has passed down to my sisters.
It is a family drama. It breaks dishes. It
runs to me with kisses, soft. And with claws.
It blooms at night also. My tiger lily. Loss.

STEVE SCAFIDI

First Warm Day in a College Town

Today is the day the first bare-chested
        runners appear, coursing down College Hill
                as I drive to campus to teach, hard

not to stare because it's only February 15,
        and though I now live in the South, I spent
                my girlhood in frigid Illinois

hunting Easter eggs in the snow,
        or trick-or-treating in the snow,
                an umbrella protecting my cardboard wings,

so now it's hard not to see these taut colts
        as my reward, these yearlings testing the pasture,
                hard as they come toward my Nissan

not to turn my head as they pound past,
        hard not to angle the mirror
                to watch them cruise down my shoulder,

too hard, really, when I await them like crocuses,
        search for their shadows
                as others do the groundhog's, and suddenly

here they are, the boys without shirts,
        how fleet of foot, how cute their buns, I have made it
                again, it is spring.

Hard to recall just now
        that these are the torsos of my students,
                or my past or future students, who every year

grow one year younger, get one year fewer
        of my funny jokes and hip references
                to *Fletch* and Nirvana, which means

some year if they catch me admiring
        the hair downing their chest, centering
                between their goalposts of hipbones,

then going undercover beneath their shorts,
        the thin red or blue nylon shorts, the fabric
                of flapping American flags or the rigid sails of boats—

some year, if they catch me admiring, they won't
        grin grins that make me, busted,
                grin back—hard to know a spring will come

when I'll have to train my eyes
        on the dash, the fuel gauge nearing empty,
                hard to think of that spring, that

distant spring, that very very very
        (please God) distant
                spring.

BETH ANN FENNELLY

Flesh of John Brown's Flesh: December 2, 1859

I dared not refuse to obey, but at first I did not strike hard.
"Harder!" he said, "harder, harder!"

—John Brown Jr.

We knew the rules and punishments:
three lashes for lack of diligence,
eight for disobeying mother
or telling lies . . . . *No blood,* he'd say,

and no remission. Came a day
he started keeping my account,
as at a store. And came another
he called me to the tannery:

a Sunday, day of settlement.
I'd paid one-third the owed amount
when he, to my astonishment,
handed the blue beech switch to me,

tearful. (The greatest of my fears:
never his whippings, but those tears.)
And so it was my father paid,
himself, the balance I had owed,

our mingled blood a token of
a thing that went unnamed: his love.
This nation, too, is his bad child.
And she has failed him, made him wild

with rage and grief, and will be scourged
nearly to death before she, purged,
may rise and stand. *No blood,* I hear
him saying still, *and no remission.*

So hang him today, Virginia; cheer
his body swaying in the air—
tomorrow you will learn what's true:
hanging's a thing he's done for you.

GEOFFREY BROCK

Floundering

1.

When the tides were right
outside of Pass Christian, I would see them
heron-stalking the shallows, gigs held high

in one hand, a lantern in the other.
They were tracking beds, depressions where flounders
had ambushed a mullet or mud minnow

and had settled back down a couple yards away,
leaving nothing behind but cloudy water
and the imprints of their bodies.

2.

They bury their bodies into the dirty bottom,
waiting for prey, accepting
the coarse sand and silt

like monks accepted hair shirts,
waited for some sign of luminous grace
to hover above them

and take their hungers away.
They expose only the black pearls
of their cattywampus eyes,

one nested between the gill plate
and jagged teeth, the other lurking
at the edge of their mottled, spade-shaped head

since the eye seeped through the body
to merge with the other
when they were just fry,

condemning them to vision always fixed
upward and to the terrible weight of the world.
Perhaps they don't scurry

when the giggers find them because they've conceded
the shallow graves of their bodies while in awe
of the light spreading above them,

and, perhaps, in those barbed seconds,
they're bucking in the ecstasy
of their flesh rising into the impaled air.

ADAM VINES

The Folklore of Waitresses

That day swallows flew from God's mouth down to earth.
They landed in the bare red oaks outside the café.
Rumor was the sounds they made stopped cars. Inside the small room
a waitress passed from table to table.
The smell of rosemary and sage fell out
of the pleats in her dress and embalmed the air
for miles around.

Behind her back, she heard the music

of people saying she looked so familiar.
On each of their plates she dropped
a handful of fresh herbs. When the people ate,
they felt fuller than they had ever felt. Their lives felt full then,
as if they would rise out of their bodies
and see themselves sitting there
with nothing to do. When she left them,

the birds broke into little flowers on the trees.

MEGAN SEXTON

Foreday in the Morning

My mother grew morning glories that spilled onto the walkway
    toward her porch
Because she was a woman with land who showed as much by
    giving it color.
She told me I could have whatever I worked for. That means she was
    an American.
But she'd say it was because she believed
In God. I am ashamed of America
And confounded by God. I thank God for my citizenship in spite
Of the timer set on my life to write
These words: I love my mother. I love black women
Who plant flowers as sheepish as their sons. By the time the blooms
Unfurl themselves for a few hours of light, the women who tend them
Are already at work. Blue. I'll never know who started the lie that we
    are lazy,
But I'd love to wake that bastard up
At foreday in the morning, toss him in a truck, and drive him under
    God
Past every bus stop in America to see all those black folk
Waiting to go to work for whatever they want. A house? A boy
To keep the lawn cut? Some color in the yard? My God, we leave
    things green.

JERICHO BROWN

Funny

Desire, she said, is a funny thing. The more you have of it the less you want it. I was enmeshed in a delicate hermeneutical adventure. What is the difference between a shock wave and a detonation, a simple matter of distance? Suddenly I remembered that most of the universe is composed of invisible material. Some particles disappear before they exist. It is very possible that memory is vestigial, useless, an appendix of aromas, tomato leaves in some childhood garden. I grew nauseated. I thought of her lungs heaving with blood under nerve-ridden bones, the imprimatur of artery throbbing in her throat like a gull in a wave. We were on vacation in a coastal city and the waters were too warm to allow us to free the lobsters we'd bought at the supermarket and could not eat. The sugar sand was the end result of repetitive violent action. I could see past the sun. The dark matter was growing like a cancer. In her brain her mind was supposed to lie. That flesh, too, was emptiness, darkness, tendrils spun like threads from green worms. There's not a damned thing funny about it, I said. Not funny ha-ha, she said. Funny like weird.

THEODORE WOROZBYT

Gas Station Restroom

The present tense
is the body's past tense
here; hence
the ghost sludge of hands
on the now gray strip
of towel hanging limp
from the jammed dispenser;
hence the mirror
squinting through grime
at grime, and the worn-
to-a-sliver of soiled soap
on the soiled sink.
The streaked bowl,
the sticky toilet seat, air
claustral with stink—
all residues and traces
of the ancestral
spirit of body free
of spirit—hence,
behind the station,
at the back end of the store,
hidden away
and dimly lit
this cramped and
solitary carnival
inversion—Paul
becoming Saul
becoming scents
anonymous
and animal; hence,
over the insides
of the lockless stall
the cave-like
scribblings and glyphs
declaring unto all

who come to it
in time: "heaven
is here at hand
and dark, and hell
is odorless; hell
is bright and clean."

ALAN SHAPIRO

Geese

Not the celebrated V
but what precedes it,
this tangle untangling
then firming itself
into a line, a card
shuffle from one hand
to the other that drops
the deck, so not order
but its impulse, the
jockeying of the not-yet-
chosen to choose the chosen,
movement without
determined purpose,
your daughter lifting
her crayon above
the paper to write words
without knowing
any letters, a scribble
until she finishes and
points and says, "There."

JAMES MAY

Ghazal for Buildings

What has fallen? A building.
What has fallen now? Another building.

His parents named him to honor the prophet,
their child who flew the plane into the building.

This Mohammed was disciple of a Saudi man
whose family had made billions in building.

We all know well how to destroy.
We know that better than we know building.

We have mastered mass destruction—dreamed it,
forged it in the heart of a five-walled building.

How much could we destroy before we see
each temple, mosque, or church is just a building?

Built to serve those who cut loss, build profit,
two towers bore the name of just one building.

When building Babel, people spoke inscrutable tongues.
It's getting close to Ramadan. The hum of prayers is building.

DAN ALBERGOTTI

Ghost Season

Hibiscus in January, the only stars
visible, furious blooms just

as the leafless banana trees jag
their way into the Houston air.

Winter evaporates here like alcohol
on a cotton swab, and left is a half

summer which will hang on until
the summer proper starts swinging

and then on into October, really,
so that fall's caterwaul is all we get:

suppressed, every season but the burning
one. Imagine a world in which

extremes lope off with the largest
shares, this near tropical hotbox.

Think of laboring to breathe inside
a sauna, a white towel soaking

with your sweat, your pores gorging
themselves like wicks, skin nearly sentient

with stinging heat and wood; think
of the rising blister from a hot skillet

stuck to skin, and you'll know how,
when she claimed her kiss from you

in front of me, I became both
humiliated autumn and igneous summer,

my ignorance at once slapped awake,
and god, I haven't seen snow in years.

MELANIE JORDAN

God Is an American

I still love words. When we make love in the morning,
your skin damp from a shower, the day calms.
Schadenfreude may be the best way to name the covering
of adulthood, the powdered sugar on a black shirt. I am

alone now on the top floor pulled by obsession, the ink
on my fingers. And sometimes it is a difficult name.
Sometimes it is like the world before America, the kin-
ship of fools and hunters, the children, the dazed dream

of mothers with no style. A word can be the boot print
in a square of fresh cement and the glaze of morning.
Your response to my kiss is *I have a cavity.* I am in
love with incompletion. I am clinging to your moorings.

Yes, I have a pretty good idea what beauty is. It survives
alright. It aches like an open book. It makes it difficult to live.

TERRANCE HAYES

Going to the Movies Alone

Tonight, I want to see something explode.
I want to see a dirty blonde
in a ripped white tank
pointing a gun at a bald man
who looks like me.
I want to see a lot less talk and a lot more action.
I want to watch a powerful man be seduced
by the wrong woman.
I want to see someone start believing in Jesus.
I want to see someone baptized
in blood and bullets and gore and gunfire.
I want to see an expensive woman in a diamond bikini
light a stick of dynamite and dive into the sea.
I want to tear through the border between dream and reality.
I want to see the American beast unleashed
in suburbia, see citizens fleeing the uncaged
monster as he storms through our city.
I want a high body count and screaming
police sirens in the chase scene.
I want to see a bomb blown onscreen in 3D.
I want to feel the flame and debris,
hear the blood-smeared Superfather say to his son,
"Everything's gonna be OK. We won."
I want to see the sun rise once again over the burnt city
before the theater lights come on
and I go out the door marked EXIT
and into the winter night, the vast
dark parking lot slick with snow and ice
where my car waits alone under a streetlight.
I clear the frost from my window,
try to unlock the frozen door.

ANSEL ELKINS

The Gothic Line

That evening I must have crossed it, racketing out
the cobbles in an orange city bus to Casalecchio—
suburb of Bologna on the Reno's banks—
to dine with those I hardly knew, owners of the only
café near the school where every day I filled blanks
with proper nouns, conjugations in the remote past,
for which, I later learned, Italian now has little use.
What was I doing as I stamped my feet, then ticket,
ascended the stairs at the stop, huddled in my half
literacy and cheap coat I had to buy
when a winter I had not counted on descended?
I must have transgressed some checkpoint
between acquaintance and friend, grim shoreline
pocked with the unintelligible artifacts
of embarrassment and xenophilia, as Mina
buzzed me up to a linen table and the foreboding
of their furniture: *mobili* in Italian, the movables,
like me on the ride out of the urban, repeating
scant vocabulary to the cobble's stutter.

And it's not the tortellini served that night, handmade,
curled in silken broth, or the fizzy wine, which Dino—
from Costante, constant, forever—bottled himself.
Not even some idea of the exotic, which surely
I still felt then, one season into my becoming,
my beginning Italian like a wounded machine
sputtering its declensions to their transnational
sympathy, which, after all, could be anyone's.
But the grandfather, who arrived after dinner,
spoke a broken dialect gauzed in bookish Italian—
another kind of wound—whose eyes,
when Mina introduced me as the American,
glazed over then burned through me,
or the version of me forever fixed in his past,
in an Allied tank entering Bologna,

while he holed up in the hills near the Gothic Line,
his wife in labor, in a shelter outside the punished
city and the periodic sentences of bombing.

And though I confess now my ignorance
of war, that I first entered the vast cathedral
of its history in Bologna that winter, still
I knew enough to understand what he didn't say,
which, in my own tongue, sounds like this:
You, who liberated the streets in your machines,
who delivered my daughter from the fire hills
and noise of our wrongness, still I claim you,
blue-eyed bringer of the marketplace.
Hold my hand, as you are doing now,
as you will continue to do, your calling,
your curse—for you will occupy forever
one person to me, constant, immovable.

CHAD DAVIDSON

Gun of Wishes

of dreams, gun that opens the mind, gun
of rewards held to the temple, gun
of desire, magic gun,
bloodless and free of catastrophe,
no blood exploding from a whorl of hair
and tissue and skull, gun
that cures, gun of innocence—that's the gun
for me—one that takes out the enemy
with bullets of care, yes, a cautious gun, gun
of considerations, gun you can carry anywhere
and no one minds your gun of good intentions.
Conscious gun, gun of a gun, gun *for you*, gun
for me, trigger-happy nation
of guns,
merry guns, guns a-go-go, guns gone
wild, dancing guns like banjoes plucked
hysterical. It's a scream these guns
we believe in. Savior guns, that will set us right,
godly guns, guns at the fount, clean as a whistle,
hot as chickens in a pot, gun for gun's sake, guns
as promised for our own protection, hunting guns,
dove-hunting guns, sweet coo of guns, guns
that will fire to war no more, yes, guns for peace,
kumbaya guns, singing guns—like shooting stars—
a lullaby riddling the night.

VIEVEE FRANCIS

Halloween

Somewhere in town tonight,
a woman is discovering
her inner Sexy Pirate.

This is not to be confused
with one's inner Sexy Witch,
Sexy Kitten, Sexy Librarian,
Sexy Bo Peep, Sexy Vampire,
Sexy Race Car Driver, or
inner Sexy Ophthalmologist.

She forgot to buy ribbon,
so she threads the corset's eyelets
with gym shoes laces.
She re-poofs the sleeves
of her buccaneer blouse.

Arrrr, she says to the mirror.
Argh, the mirror sighs in return.

Once I asked my mother why
anyone would wear tights like that
to net a fish.
Wouldn't your legs get cold?
Wouldn't your heels slip
on the wet deck of a ship? *Shush*,

my mother said, adjusting the wig
on her Sexy Cleopatra.

Somewhere in town tonight,
a sitter sets out the pumpkin.
A girl studies its fat head.
They punch its eyes in, so
it can see. They cut its mouth out,

so it can smile. *Now you bring it*

to life, the sitter will say.
And where its seeds had been,
the girl will place a flame.

SANDRA BEASLEY

Homecoming

My father hated it. And worse, the washed-out stars
burning the local headlines, who went as far
as graduation, then to work—grinding out hours
on their heels, rerunning dropped passes, sour
dip spit in their frowns. Today, pro-grade turf
hides scabs of sod on which we flipped-off curfew,
kicking empties through the uprights. My friends
are boosters now, and fathers: model citizens
who swapped the scoreboard's bulbs for LEDs.
My name never graced its sad, blinking vacancy.
Distance, my painter friend says, creates an illusion
of perspective. Beyond the ads for Verizon
wasn't him, but me, back after years away.
I scanned crumbling stands for the face of a boy
who bayed at other boys, a stitch of shadow
that I once was: a self I barely recognized, but knew
as much as I know him, like football and fall.
As anyone knows one's father. Hardly at all.

ERIC SMITH

Horse and Rider

Sing unto the Lord a drift of a song,
a song that goes before the Law:

make of your voice a shaft of flame
shifting into cloud and back again,

a rift in a wave, a crack in a wheel,
a road in the midst of the sea;

make of your voice a staff turned snake
turned brass turned tambourine.

Sing of swift colts bolting
from their mares onto the plains of tender sand,

bolts of dyed silk rippling as they unfurl—
cedar, sable, silver, sunset, snow.

Sing of the vacant stables, the casks of grain;
of the rakes and forks that lean against the stalls;

of the stable-boys—all younger sons—
whose charges charge away.

Sing of helmets hailed upon the fields,
gold flax and barley rotting in the bud;

of the bare-headed boys who urge their chariots on
with surging throats: O sing of their black hair.

Sing of the groomed hooves and flanks
and haunches brushed blinding in the glare,

jolting the riders they bear—all younger sons—
until the sand tenders itself unto the sea.

Sing this day of the gift of the Lord: the genesis
of a song so old it has no attribution;

of a tongue's first poetry—the gleaming shard
which broke from prose, from simple speech,

the jagged line which founded epic, identity, belief.
Sing of defeat, for without defeat, how could we sing?

Sing of swords, shields, chariots, sifting
down beneath the tangling reeds.

Sing of the clear dry heavens, the mottled sea—
cedar, sable, silver, sunset, snow.

Sing unto the Lord, for He has triumphed gloriously;
He has slaughtered whom He has slaughtered;

He has shown Himself worthy of all our noise:
He has rid the earth of a few more horses, a few more boys.

MELISSA RANGE

How We Count In The South

      Add one
tonight, when the barred owl
calls her tent revival, the cortege
trailing a mosquito truck's
deodorant breeze.
      Plus two, the night
before, where they inject one more
black man up the road in Georgia.
The Supreme Court tweets his final
opinion.
      Which leads to three:
Dear Jesus, The Reason
For Each Season, of course we're
exhausted by our soul's litigation,
the old ones still milling at the polling
place, the recently deceased sweating
their subpoenas in feckless hands.
      Required to appear,
we wait. We nurse ourselves and take
a number. We lean against the sneeze
guards at the country buffet until our
ankles swell.
      Please. Don't tell us
history. Nobody hearts a cemetery
like we do,
      where re-enactors wad
their muskets between headstones,
and ancient belles in neck-high silk
prepare for the previously fought
war. Every day is a day before.
      Though we do hear
the news. Oh sure. It gets to us.
Story is, up north, people shit
crushed pineapple and rest stop
whores give change with paper

money. Story is inscribed, fixed as
the roulette wheels clacking inside
casinos, where party boats freak
like viscous bath toys in this
electric gulf.
       Certainly, we've learned
our numbers. We build a church for
anyone who owns a pair of knees.
But still, the old disease is catching,
      so pray with us—
           Unplug the power, Lord.
           Illuminate the devils. Degrease
               the righteous man's eye.

ERIN BELIEU

Human Imprint

The baby vulture, captured,
imagined me as I was:
mother, lover, rival.

Call it an existential crisis.
The nest I'd found
out prowling the woods

should never have fallen,
but it nearly
fell into my arms.

A real mother hovered
upwards, rocked
on the thin air above the river.

Call it a moral quandary
if you must, but just
think about it first:

the very first thing effective
at love she saw,
yes, was me.

Think positive psychology.
All this vulture
could learn about nurture

I taught her: how to laugh
like a drunk in the afternoons,
how to touch

softly the back of a neck.
And nature:
that jealousy is rage,

but rage like passion, dies down.
Once, set free,
she rebuffed the hospitable air.

Call her scatterbrained,
purblind.
I named her Angeline,

and Angeline limped back
to my doorstep and pecked
at my backdoor glass.

When I shot her, her neck
writhed like a rattlesnake
alive in the grass.

HASTINGS HENSEL

Hush

Cries of katydids make a pool of sound,
      filling up the invisible bowl of night, whose
sill you rest on, spelled by stars' faint light.
      Now the pestle moon will grind your troubles
down to thinnest powder against the grooves of
      those coarse cries, and now a chirring wind sends
trials to pasture, scatters them past the fence.
      You remain. Slide down that singing surface,
spilling into it, like the black-eared kitten,
      who, once she has eaten, steps into the blue
porcelain bowl, curls up, and never thinking
      she herself could be eaten, sleeps and sleeps.

ANNA LENA PHILLIPS BELL

Hutch

—by way of what they say

From back when it was Nam time I tell you what.
Them days men boys gone dark groves rose like Vietnam bamboo.
Aftergrowth something awful.
Green have mercy souls here seen camouflage everlasting.
Nary a one of the brung-homes brung home whole.

Mongst tar-pines come upon this box-thing worked from scrapwood.
Puts me much myself in mind of a rabbit-crouch.
Is it more a meat-safe.
Set there hid bedded there looking all the world like a coffin.
Somebody cares to tend to it like a spring gets tendered clears the leaves!

Whosoever built it set wire window-screen down the sides.
Long about five foot or thereabouts close kin to a dog-crate.
A human would have to hunch.
Closes over heavy this hingey-type lid on it like a casket.
Swearing to Jesus wadn't it eye-of-pine laid down for the floor.

Remembering the Garner twins Carl and Charlie come home mute.
Cherry-bombs 4th of July them both belly-scuttling under the house.
Their crave of pent-places ditchpipes.
Mongst tar-pines come upon this box-thing worked from scrapwood.
From back when it was Nam time I tell you what.

ATSURO RILEY

I Believe in Pain the Way Others Believe in God

for M. O.

I don't experience god,
says Michael, his cheeks glowing
in the café's weak light. *I think*
I will always be lonely,
he tells me. As we talk,
I can't piece his face together.
I see him the way Picasso painted
the woman wearing a hat,
all angles and fragments.
My hands look thin, and I think
I might be slowly disappearing.
He says, *I go into a crowded room*
and feel all the pain. I wonder,
does god make a noise we can't hear?
I worry about this friend of mine,
who is quiet, sad. I'd ask god,
"Do you like holding us
by the throat?" Michael asks,
How can people live with all that pain?
Later, a shabby man
clutching a bottle of whiskey
crosses in front of my car.
There's a stoplight, a woman
inside a building practicing
piano. It's so easy to get confused:
driving, stopping to buy milk,
then I look up, and it's raining,
and my flight from Detroit
to New Orleans has landed.
Factories dim behind gumbo
and Dixieland, and I'm donning
several strings of beads, one white,

one blue, one violet, like in a postcard
for tourists, but I'm not smiling
standing beside a park bench,
a statue of a soldier missing an arm.

BETH GYLYS

I Had a Little Cash

I had a little cash and I was going to buy a gun
but they said, No, you can't
They said, Believe in the police
We believe in the police
All you have to do is call them
They come running, running
I had a little cash to buy a gun
but they said, Why would you do that
Who are you to do that
We do not do that with our money
I want to raise a goat in a field
and protect the goat from a lion
If it's about animals, then may I buy a gun?
I had the cash to buy the gun
but they said, You can't you're a poet
Poets don't buy guns
So I dressed with my empty leather holster
(in truth I was thinking of some poets
just South of here who go shooting
I know I am not alone), and wore my holster
over my blue jeans and said to them
What do you want me to do
Should I wait for something fatal to happen
Oh, you want me to run
You want me to gun-less run leg-less across a field
Are you trying to get me killed

JILLIAN WEISE

The Illusionist

Without the usual work of wands,
she dazzles solely with her hands.

The coin behind your ear is gone.
Her turtledoves have turned to stone.

She plucks the rose from her corsage,
your ring tucked in its petaled cage.

She knows your card. She levitates.
The coin appears in duplicates.

And though she makes a show of it—
the scripted struggle, the long wait—

no locks or chains are sound enough
to bind her to this stage. And though

you know the limits of the eye,
her sleight of hand, the hidden lie,

you choose to see as through a sieve.
You still applaud. You still believe.

MICHAEL SHEWMAKER

In/exhaustible

The billboards into town advertise Southern Gun
& Pawn, Slot Cars, say Everyone's Preapproved!
Best Deal on a Home, Period—the prefabs that come

in halves on the back of trucks labeled WIDE LOAD,
and this was a manufacturing town, until the factories
closed up shop, the warehouses turned to churches

with food pantries, roadways littered with signs:
Are Your Bills Crippling You? Psalm 75:1. Ferguson
Tire: We Buy Gold, then Welcome to Martinsville—

A City Without Limits says the sign on the road in,
and there behind the rows of shotgun houses, a dye plant,
abandoned, two mottled smokestacks rising like goalposts,

no longer pumping out anything of worth near the sign
that says Bankruptcy Could Be Your Solution (All Welcome),
the sign that says We Love You Pastor. Get Well Soon.

The sign says cash for old broken jewelry, and this
is a town where everyone's broke or gone. It is
Christmastime in Martinsville, and Santa in his red robes,

in his Shriner's hat, stands regal and fat in the darkened
consignment store. Molded sheep rest on cotton batting
near a nest made from hay. The faded wise men kneel

with hands clasped, gazing at that baby with outstretched arms.
In another window, lit-up swaying snowmen sharing a hymnal,
and the plastic baby rests among doves, nestled by a lady

in blue robes with her head bowed. This is a city
of supplication, of duct-taped and empty storefronts,
of faded holiday ornaments, where downtown businesses

only open three days a week—a city that left its smokestacks
raised in prayer to the signs, and the sign says Highest Prices
Paid in Cash, says HUGE furniture & mattress sale.

Some billboards quote a politician: "Attracting New Jobs"
but the local radio talk show has callers buzzing, all asking
the same question: when is our train gonna come in when

is our train comin' in where is that train and can you hear it
in the peeling storefronts, the empty storage facilities,
the degree-completion joints? The walk-ins welcome,

the spider-webbed glass, the abandoned call centers?
People speak of your wonderful deeds. The plastic families
wear wire halos, and fold their arms to wait and wait.

Someone will bring work. The smokestacks
are out of breath. The sign at Lays It Away
says Happy Thanksgiving to All and God Bless.

ERIKA MEITNER

In the Beginning, Death

The man named his wife Eve, because she would become
the mother of all the living.

—Genesis 3:20

I enter,
a type of Adam:
   one greasy sparerib
touched by God,
all Amazon (taller, even!),
   approach strident,
lashing his ears like a fallen angel.

Astride an altered ocean
   (*this* is timelessness),
mountainous with salt,
   I look for clear water.
Overhead, the first black nights beat their wings,
   hesitant to fly.

Portable, I'm meager,
a dented can
in God's taxonomy of liabilities.
   Woe.
This should be paradise.

   My heart stiffens
   like a moldy rind.
More like God than ever,
I'll plant my son in the ground,
fill cracked jars with water,
   and scrape my way across the sharpened earth.

Lo and behold, as a comet curves
the sooty rim of night,

as one who serves,
I may rest in familiar flights.

NATALIE GRAHAM

Ink

Is there a canvas crueler than the body?
The ink is permanent. The skin is not.
I have no patience for the lover's gaudy
heart—swollen, pierced—a hackneyed blot
beating against the odds. I've seen them all:
straddled by seraphim, or torn apart—
on women, men, the lesser parlor's wall—
hallmarked MOM, or skewered by a dart
from Cupid's quiver.
                           But enough of love.
I work in monochrome. I deal in skulls.
Behind each piece a brief, familiar story.
It ends in bones—the sort of plot that dulls
the point. My needle's steadiest above
a stinging script that reads:
                           Memento Mori.

MICHAEL SHEWMAKER

Intersection

In the front yard, red,
limp azaleas,
in silent litany,
cluster for water.

Magnolia blossoms
shrivel, yellow.
Shrieking crickets scuttle
behind a battered mailbox.

As summer persists,
everything exaggerates.

Light splits darkened corners,
lines the wooden floor.
Selfish and unashamed,
I am jealous of your better daughter.

Even in August,
when I'd expect winter to hide
beneath the ground,
you look cold,

trembling and glittering
like some weak thing of God.

I spoon you diminished bites.
Smaller, you say.

Your stiff fingers, like matchsticks,
scatter across the sheet.

Though your body is a battleship
upon which night advances,

could you pity me, Mother,
cornered and nicked as a doorstop?

NATALIE GRAHAM

Introduction to Home Economics

I'm not convinced my mother ever forgave me
for carving, instead of the jack-o-lantern, the hand
she used to steady it in her lap. We sat
on the porch with a kitchen knife, newspapers spread
beneath us. The pumpkin's skin was stubborn, my mother
left-handed. I was six, my mantra *Let me try*.
Then blood and blood and blood. Then tourniquets
of towels and the rush to the E.R.,
my father driving. I stayed behind with a neighbor,
my mother returning with black stitches, her hand
wrapped like a mummy's, to finish the face we'd started.
Each Halloween, she brought it up again,
reminding me what I had done, how I had hurt her,
though she was the one who handed me the knife.

CHELSEA RATHBURN

Jeremiad

A baby, not ours, crying at the movies,
or a sermon lozenge-wrapper wracked:
the world frowns upon disturbance

as it does an unsightly mole
or a patch of skin scaled and broken
on a hand or unfortunate face.

And the phone's bell in the night, its fracture
so jagged the bones of disaster show
through the skin of sleep torn and regrown.

For every messenger coiling through the wire
and every journey jackknifed,
now I take back the remainder:

limbs basketed, littered apples back to the tree
so growth commences audibly
like a choir's warming-up hum;

and back to furs the prince in the cell,
back the book I was reading when it got burned.
Now we'll finish the talks we started.

I'll make you say all you wanted,
and our possibilities sprout like stumps

the way it should have been in the house
with its wings rebuilt on the mountain
ore-stripped long ago—all of it—

lives led by our shadows—
the people our parents almost married
father us, the stream uninterrupted

diverges; every patient comes unstrung
from his gurney—but it's just too hard.
I want it all.

MELANIE JORDAN

Jungle Fever Epithalamium

Dearly beloved, can we call it this?
I've never left the States. We'll have the kiss.

The unity candle is just a guise?
Pronounce me wife, him groomed to colonize?

It won't happen like that. (So what.) He's white.
(Who cares?) I'm black. For me, a savage night

Is zigzagging, drunk, on a downtown street.
My hair is natural. I like my meat

Pink in the middle. Known to piggy back
July, I sop heat up like a biscuit. Smack

Is shit, shit right. Thirty and never caught
DWB, some random policeman ought

To let me get profiled.
                                    Is that a yes?
I did know Randall Kenan, I confess,

Before I met him. (We still have those set
Meetings on Wednesdays.) I know I'd forget

When Dad clanned up, got him a kilt, and made
Us see those bagpipes if I could. (We paid

For that.) My god. When *Malcolm X* was ten
At the Cineplex, I read Haley, and, then

Wore red and black and green—all proud, thick-skinned.
Mom said, "You know that you're from Maryland."

Is that a no, long-lost fraternal twin,

Black to my white? There'll be no Lohengrin

Chorus. No conga line. The rhythm will
Not get you. No. No dollar, dollar bill,

Y'all. It is not electric. Throw the rice.
Snuff out the unity candle. Let ice

Sculptures crack like the streets of Baltimore.
Bring on the wedding night. I'm ready for

The morning after.
                    Hon, hug out my spleen,
Crush all my bones. Position me and lean

My body up against the naked trees
Interred in summer love's transparencies

Drifting us through the threshold. Please. Unpin
My hair. I'm wild for your obsidian.

ERICA DAWSON

Kismet

Our limbs in such
        ligature
that, world adjourned,
would even God have recognized

us as human?
        A swallowing.
Then pearling scree at the sill
Of—where?—me

or a tree shivering
        with wings?
O light jacket of the air!
I know your hand was—there—

a place impossible, else,
        to open
to the light
& survive. Years

this way,
        sun drifting by
on a raft of shadow.
Un-asylumed breathing.

What doesn't love
        restraint?
I felt divinity pour itself
into your body's icon—& live.

LISA RUSS SPAAR

Lampblack

Black as a charred plum-stone, as a plume
from a bone-fire, as a flume of ravens
startled from a battle-tree—this lantern resin
the monk culls from soot to quill the doom
and glory of the Lord won't fade. The grime
of letters traced upon the riven
calf-skin gleams dark as fresh ash on a shriven
penitent, as heaven overawing time.
World's Glim, Grim Cinderer, is it sin
or history or a whimsied hex that burns
all life to tar? We are dust, carbon
spilled out from your Word, a lamp overturned
into the pit of pitch beneath your pen,
the inkhorn filled before the world was born.

MELISSA RANGE

The Landlocked Lighthouse

I see its signal swing above the trees,
while driving through a storm in Tennessee.
It slices sideways, turning in the night,
and lends to someone, somewhere sense of sight.
Where does it lead? I doubt I'll ever know.
But I suspect it's where lost people go.
I would not follow if I knew the source.
I've marked my map and shouldn't change my course.
Though, I'll admit I find a certain charm
in parking the car and putting on my warm
blue coat, then drifting off into the green,
like a fisherman for fish he's never seen—
who finds himself adrift, alone; his chart
wet from the rain, the only thing apart
from all the dark: the swinging of a lamp.
Though here there is no sea, just leaves and damp
soil, musky, smelling of mushrooms and mold,
like something living, fresh, but very old.
And out there, calling, is the tower's swinging
light, calling clearly as a siren's singing.
I'd like to climb those tightly spiraled stairs
and find the one who tends to the affairs
of wanderers turned searchers in the dark,
present my map, and have him make the mark.

CHAD ABUSHANAB

Layover

I have half a mind to make a move.

I stayed in Archer City where
I made Larry McMurtry proud
By downing one too many shots
Of ice-cold vodka, tumbler-sized.
I hollered every word of "Sweet
Home Alabama" while the band
Reprised "Knockin' on Heaven's Door,"
Packed up, and quit the Legion dance.

I thought I didn't know that song.

I two-stepped with a cowboy, kissed
A Yankee (wrong), regretted it,
So found my cowboy once again:
The Yankee looking like a young
Paul Newman and the cowboy like
I'll bed you, hard and hot in jeans.

What was it in the Texas air
That brought Delilah out of me?
Was it the quail and wild hogs?
The BBQ cooked from a cow
That tasted like a slaughtered cow?

What hiked my temperature? It climbed
The diving board and took its clothes
Off, piece by piece, as if last May
Were my last picture show, last chance
To sweat with strangers in a Spur
Hotel room, quaint with double beds
And Byron on the table, me
As Cybil Shepherd in the lights
For the first time, marking the stage,

Walking in beauty like the night
Too much for such a little place
Where the town Indian said she
Was the town Indian; and, my
Sweet cowboy said I gave him eyes,
Said I was high-heeled trouble, said

I have the tendency to lead.

ERICA DAWSON

Lines

tell me
the smooth box
rendered by the gloved
hands of a mime

tell me
the spinning particles
between your foot and my foot
each propped on the railing
tell me that nervous inch

tell me yellow
that lines up nevertheless
perennials burning
for their lost house

tell me oxygen
from a cooler layer
unsuitable for
the breath you must take
to tell me

I've scripted
your intimate talk in my head
speak it back

tell me
white butcher paper
the tongue wrapped
separate from the heart

JULIE FUNDERBURK

Lonely

A ladder on a limb, not even wind
among green leaves. A tin can, rust-lipped

on a steam grate. A bag caught in a bare tree.
Wires. Stand of evergreens. Snow.

The furnace clicking on in the deep of the night.
A buzzard tree ruffling in the breeze. Mole shuffle.

Bullfrog quiet in the pickerel weed.
Street turning onto empty street.

A lover, woken, saying, "I am asleep."
A highway sighing all day long.

A bleating sheep. The dropped key;
the tongue as it meets the back of the teeth.

You, you and me. A beloved body gone
and whom, whom to tell it to?

Rosary beads hung on the bed post.
Mary, dear Mary. Her white lily.

Somewhere, a child dreams fitfully.
A mother locks the windows, shuts off the lights.

There's a cough at the end of a hospital corridor.
A dock on a lake. A gutted fish. A hook.

A spoon. The moon. A bone.
God in thought on his golden road.

MELANIE ALMEDER

Love Song with Exiles

November. The devil's keys
dangle from its neck.
The dry leaves we step on
look like small hands
missing thumb and index finger.

Men in other countries feel its dampness,
see its black stain like a shawl on chickens
scurrying to their coops.
These men have no land
and the land of others remains quiet and pale
like a face adrift in a casket.

Here, the night dies of cirrhosis.
Two months and your dogs still wait for you
as if waiting for daybreak.
Your mother brings me soup
on Sundays and fills my forehead with kisses.
Once she brought me a handful of snow
and left her pulse in the embers to keep me warm.
I'll survive, I said,
and when she said your name,
her tongue turned to foam.

In other countries, the dry cough that rises
from the hearts of women
has no choice
but to hang itself.
Through holes in the walls,
the women watch their men fold
goodbyes like pieces of paper.

The men promise to return,
but even their names will be erased
by the drizzle falling on the pavement.

Their women will never sell their babies.
Babies sucking their thumbs.
Babies so small you could carry them in purses.

OCTAVIO QUINTANILLA

Master of None

Turn the bottle not the cork.
I want a draft on my desk by morning.
Knuckles to the blade. A quick punch
to its bottom flaps opens an empty box.
On top of the stack, a bottle twisted flowers the napkins.
Alternating the direction of end wood
keeps the pile from falling. Pat your palm
on the metal to gauge the heat.
Marry the bottles. Count the till. Spray the mats.
Last one out turns out the lights.

First one in gets their pick of the papers.
Look for the pot in the panty drawer.
Don't put all you've got into a single hole:
it will be a day of ditches. Bend from your knees.
Breathe deep. Never carry sheetrock before the wind.
A little vinegar poured into a bucket of water
will do the floor just fine. A cigarette pack
in the shirt pocket justifies the break.
Lefty loosey, righty tighty. Round hole,
square peg. I quit.

There are the things you know by doing.
You pick up what you can from expert hands.
Herbs dry best on old window screens.
The sharpened pencil prices the book.
Wet the knife before the slice or a little cake remains.
Tamp the grounds light but firm.
Time your orders to fit the rush.
And, if all else fails, having served the meal
out of order, delivered the wrong drinks,
free deserts all around maintains the level of the tip.

SEBASTIAN MATTHEWS

Matches

Red-faced, arguing briefly
their one point against the night,

or blackened, sober as blown
light bulbs, they weigh more

in the eye than the hand.
Infernal dragonflies,

their wings pinched off.
Informal flames on crutches.

I work a fresh match
like a needle to sew a gown

of blue fire for the chandelier.
I grip the spent match

like a pen, signing my soot
to this debt and that one.

The matches' testament—
which includes the diary

of an arsonist's slender apprentice,
her virginity like a fistful

of tinder—is the history of glory
in the language of ash.

They stutter, and still
they are eloquent.

GEORGE DAVID CLARK

Memorial Day

He left me with a hundred unpacked boxes
too heavy to lift up the rented stairs,
the baby, fussy with yeast, just beginning
to teethe, her first ear infection
coming on. The only calls the bill collectors',
only bills in the mail and shiny magazines
filled with pottery I wanted but couldn't buy.
I wouldn't eat for two days so my dogs could.

This was after the fifth kicked garbage can,
the kitchen a mess hall of spilled beans
and coffee grounds, after the hard right
to the ear, the rug burn, the bitten fingers,
after the crushed turtle under his boot.
I wanted to go back to Mississippi,
but I had too many dogs, cats, a newborn.
He threatened to kill whomever I left behind.

A year later, a reporter from *The Citizen*
will interview him. A reward for his purple heart,
he'll get a hero's *hip, hip, hooray!*
down at Schooner Wharf, the old bait
and tackle where he'll gas up his new outboard.
He'll wear a camouflage cap and his Ford
will sport ribbons and bands of honor.

DANIELLE SELLERS

Michael Jordan

I

Wasn't it the way he stopped dead
at the top of the key
in the thick of a fast break
as physics carried every human
defender past him in a blur—
even our eyes trained on 23
had to back up to center him—
the ball palmed like a yo-yo
in his hand and us agape
at how his knees didn't buckle,
ankle wouldn't snap in its pivot,
how he never even needed arms
to draw circles in the air
for balance like the rest of us
(walking a drunk line
or falling backwards in a pool)—
the trick of his equilibrium
and each motive to score
soothsaid by his tongue
lolling the rim of his lip
like a logo or swished net.

II

Was there ever anyone
so unmoved by gravity,
so happy in this air
between wax and rafter
at the top of the key, this firmament
he ascended for each jump shot and hung
until that cruel gravity
he never endorsed
unwinged his opponent,
dropped him to the earth

like a deviled seraph.
And how he'd unhinge
the lever of his wrist
like he was waving at someone small
or far beneath him, his eyes fixed
on the rim, his tongue, dry as nylon,
readied for the small meal of three,
and how then he'd slake a blessing of sweat
onto the limbs of those fouling below.

AUSTIN HUMMELL

Midafternoon

Walking the empty house
after a friend has gone—
nosy in my own space,
watching the rooms return,

slowly resettling
into their daily selves,
as if, seen by other eyes,
the floor, the chairs and shelves,

the paths I walk between them
and objects on them show
the brighter, clearer form—
here shabbiness, here halo—

they wear for those who visit,
for eyes that don't expend
as much sight on their sight
and see the sum of them

not dimmed by repetition,
not clotted with contempt.
In these now-hallowed rooms,
however full, unkempt,

I want to rest, to float—
a dust mote in a beam
of light squared by a window—
to sigh and lilt between

the object and the eye,
before the day can catch me
back up into myself,
and through that prism, watch me:

as I am in the house,
as I am, of the rooms—
as, in another's kinder eyes,
what had been dull dust gleams.

ANNA LENA PHILLIPS BELL

Milledgeville Haibun

Beat. Beat. Beats beat here. The sound of the train on the Georgia road, the measured claps of the wheels at the gaps of the joints of the rails is the beat of the hammer on iron and anvil at the smithy, Sol's shop, shaping shoes for mules and horses; and the sizzle of red metal in water is the train's whistle, and all echoes resound and effuse, and the last word returns like watermelons here with summer heat, beat with a hammer, beat when he, a boy, broke into the garden at the county jail at night when the beat men were asleep because theirs were the sweetest, so bust one open, the dull thud just before the crack, and eat the heart and move on to the next; and he moved on to women and settled eventually on one and finally busted her with finality, thud before crack, and he measured time raising the sweetest watermelons for a time and time served he returned, a man, and he lay on the tracks of the Georgia road cradled by the rails. Heart stopped.

> Old railroad, abandoned—
> between crossties trees grow,
> a feral pig roots below branches.

SEAN HILL

Mississippian

Once the plows had turned over
last year's corn stobs, they lay
tumbled like bad teeth
in the field's dark mouth.
Among them, arrowheads and knives,
the rarer axes, and the abundant
castoffs knapped centuries ago
shined unmistakable
as a friend's face among strangers
or the white shock of potatoes
spade-cleaved and brought to light.
It was to discover that your life
was not your own after all,
to find such a thing out there
on the hills above bottomland,
the prison farther out by the river
with its rolled-wire fences,
the fertilizer tanks like downed moons
and the great skeins of snow geese
gone for the year.
To hold the smooth cool stone
in the hand—*ubi sunt*—and hope
to conjure the crossed leather lashings
that held them to ash handles,
to think of the knapper himself
wrapped in a foul wet hide,
sullen in his crouch,
the rain drumming around him
as he chipped dreams
from a common stone
and lit a door in the dark
with even these his daytime sparks.

PAUL BONE

Moonflowers

Tonight at dusk we linger by the fence
round the garden, watching the wound husks
of moonflowers unclench themselves slowly,
almost too slow for us to see their moving—
you notice only when you look away
and back, until the bloom decides,
or seems to decide, the tease is over,
and throws its petals backward like a sail
in wind, a suddenness about this as though
it screams, almost the way a newborn screams
at pain and want and cold, and I still hear
that cry in the shout across the garden
to say another flower is about to break.
I go to where my daughter stands, flowers
strung along the vine like Christmas lights,
one not yet lit. We praise the world by making
others see what we see. So now she points and feels
what must be pride when the bloom unlocks itself
from itself. And then she turns to look at me.

JAMES MAY

Moonrise

An impossible orange moon
slimmed with two days' waning
creeps over the wan horizon

as I drive the five hours home
from the Albuquerque airport
this Easter night, my wife

asleep on the back seat.
For a minute the disk appears
to rest at the end of the road,

a final destination,
and I half expect a sign:
moon 36 miles.

Heavy and stolid, it lolls
like the flat, round stone
that sealed the tomb of Christ

in the picture Bible I had
as a child and read religiously,
as others read comic books,

and yet it seems weightless as space,
as air, this moon, this lunar
optical illusion

floating into the sky
as Earth turns in her sleep.
The hours pass, and it grows

smaller but brighter, not orange
but now the color of eggs
before my two nephews dyed them

last night. Eleven o'clock,
too late now to call my mother,
assure her that we're safe,

though she will lie awake,
draped in the haze of her fears
of missed flights, delays, or worse.

I still remember how
she woke us every Easter:
He is risen! To which we said

He is risen indeed! and we dashed
past her to the den,
knowing the resurrection

also meant chocolate bunnies
in the pastel plastic baskets
Dad stored in the attic.

Where are those photos she took
each year of my clip-on tie,
my sister's ridiculous hat?

Or of the year at my aunt's,
a family of live rabbits
hopping from a hole in their yard?

Those pictures—stuffed in a shoebox?
Or lost, thrown out by mistake,
discarded during a move?

Maybe sometimes we get it
right by accident,
trade mementos for memories

and mystery. By midnight,
the moon overhead is tiny,
a flat, white wafer,

            or the distant, secret home
        of a comic book hero
    boys conjure in their dreams.

            Or a cratered satellite
        held in orbit by its nearness
    to our planet's greater mass.

            But watching it now I recall
        from Eucharist this morning
    the dry, plain starch of the Host—

            like flour and cardboard mixed
        with the salt from a drop of sweat—
    as it broke apart in my mouth.

            And I see it whole again,
        shining like an oiled wound
    in the night sky's side.

BRENT NEWSOM

Morning, Minnesott

—*Pamlico Sound, North Carolina*

It is morning and the pelicans are filling the sky; they glide past in
    silence—stare at the choppy river below.

The right cuff of my pants is soaked as we walk up the beach
    together.

I say "together" but she is far ahead of me—slender and fleet—a
    spring doe skimming the sand.

The game we play is an ancient one—you know the name, you
    made the rules.

A crab at the edge of the pier clacks his blue claws and scowls—
    hungry to escape the sweet warm wash of nostalgia.

And the gulls diving from the sky are maniacal—compelled by greed,
    they fall—gleaming white missiles of laughter and tears.

She is so far ahead of me now that I plan for tomorrow.

The pelicans—ugly with patience & wisdom—glide gently past.

The hungover fishermen finish their coffee, pull on their rubber boots.

Around the bend, the ferry churns the dark water white—gives
    three long bellows of its horn.

TERRY KENNEDY

Moving (Again)

Trimmed hedges, flower beds and the groomed lawns
Grow smaller in the silver of the mirror.
The neighbors waving from their grim garage,
They, too, diminish first, then disappear.
They will go on about their busy lives.
They'll trim the hedge. They'll clean the grim garage.
Those old friends will continue grilling out.
They'll drink the frosty beer at sunset
As the great tectonic plates of August bronze
Slide quietly to nightshade on their lawns.

There will be talk and gossip just the same
While I, some several states away, begin
To read the long last chapter of a book,
Or walk the dog, or settle in for sleep.
Who knows what they will say. I should suppose
That they will mention me. And I may be,
To some, a fondly recollected thought.
Good-humored. Well-respected. Loyal.
Though in the grillsmoke-sweetened summer dusk,
To others, surely not.

DANIEL ANDERSON

My Father Explains the History of Sugar, the Middle Passage and Slavery to My Brother, Age 5, over Breakfast

The history of sugar is the history of skin.
Consider this bowl, filled with sugar.
This glass, filled with milk.
Your body, the value of the body—
filled with all you can make of it.
Would you trade that body for sugar
when you hunger, or the milk
when you thirst? How about someone
else, your sister, another body?

Say you wouldn't.
Know you would.

TJ JARRETT

My Lovely Assistant

After the episode of *That's Incredible!*
in which a whole family of Armenians
in sequined shirts ate fire
and spewed blue, burning plumes, my brother
tied a cottonball to a bent coathanger
and dipped the end in gasoline.

What made us who we are,
one crazy, fearless—one always afraid?
I stood by the ping-pong table
in our mother's only sparkly dress,
playing the role of *Patricia, Lovely Assistant*

because he was bigger than me,
and a master of the headlock,
and threatened, with his breath of snot
and bubble gum and cigarettes,
a vicious wedgy if I didn't.

So I handed him the silver Zippo,
not knowing what future waited for my brother,
still thinking I could save him
who hated being saved—

who took my dare one night to lie
on the yellow stripe of Brown's Bridge Road
and stayed there talking to himself,
pointing to a satellite adrift among the stars,
while I begged him to get up.

Who sat in an upstairs bedroom
giggling at the click of our father's .38.
Who loved the sting of the torch
sizzling his spit-glazed tongue.

So I kept one eye on the door, knowing
from experience how it would end,
how all things turned finally to anger
in that house, where he leaned back, shark-eyed,
and took a swig from the red gas can,
the spitting image of our father in a rage.

He stood between me and that pain.
Knowingly, he raised the magic wand up to his lips.
I sit and wonder what it means—
my brother's sweet face
bursting into flames.

PATRICK PHILLIPS

My Mother Told Us Not to Have Children

She'd say, Never have a child you don't want.
Then she'd say, Of course, I wanted you
once you were here. She's not cruel. Just practical.
Like a kitchen knife. Still, the blade. And care.
When she washed my hair, it hurt; her nails
rooting my thick curls, the water rushing hard.
It felt like drowning, her tenderness.
As a girl, she'd been the last
of ten to take a bath, which meant she sat
in dirty water alone; her mother in the yard
bloodletting a chicken; her brothers and sisters
crickets eating the back forty, gone.
Is gentleness a resource of the privileged?
In this respect, my people were poor.
We fought to eat and fought each other because
we were tired from fighting. We had no time
to share. Instead our estate was honesty,
which is not tenderness. In that it is
a kind of drowning. But also a kind of air.

REBECCA GAYLE HOWELL

My Mother Woke a Rooster

She wasn't surprised, that morning by the stove,
when she cracked open a fresh brick of coffee,
with hands feathered as the bed from which she rose.
She stood there. Upon her head, the morning sun
soothed her like guitars strumming—a halo: saint:
fit for lit candle on the mantle, the dressing table.

When she walked to the sink for water,
a bouquet of blue and black and rose
rose from the coccyx, up and over like a waterfall,
swiping the sugar and cream from the counter.
She was amazed by her wide presence in the tiny kitchen,
the incredible strength in her thighs, the ease of the strut.

In a pan hanging above the stove, she caught
the reflection of herself and swooped her rubbery
coxcomb back, letting it fall over her brow.
She pursed her red lips; her mouth just visible
deep inside a sharp beak.

She watched, in wonder, the staccatoed swivel
of her neck, rubbing what the night before
was the wrinkled throat of an old woman.
Her eyes now fitting on the face of a fighting cock.
Her red-tipped toes now claws and rough as a rope.

LAURIE ANN GUERRERO

Nails

are held in the mouth
of a gun and splinter pines
or stab flashing, metal superior
in its point. They get hit
or pounded to hold up
collector plates or families.
Our house's nails recognize
one another in their sharpness,
know the weight they carry—
they will outlast us,
and the timbers above us,
those little pikes cleaving
one to another as you
sleep on your side,
and I lie awake in our bed
while what is between us
gathers, galvanizes
into something I can strike.

KATIE CHAPLE

Neither

Her eyes flared like torches. She couldn't understand
how she'd struck me dumb. She couldn't believe,
she said, how I could believe nothing, wouldn't accept
that I would choose annihilation, death over life.

(That's what she said: *death over life*. Said it was a choice.)
She told me her lord stood and knocked and waited
for me to open a door. *It's really a simple choice*, she said.
Everlasting life or eternal death. Which one do you want?

Her eyes flared like torches carried by monks
or by villagers. Her words seemed to float
from her mouth, and her teeth were beautiful.
Isn't that strange, that teeth can be beautiful?

Have you ever looked at a mouth and thought,
Those teeth are beautiful? Have you ever looked at a skull
and thought, *Those teeth are beautiful?* Have you ever thought
about the teeth of a crocodile tearing at the flesh

of an early mammal, crushing bones and flashing white
against primordial mud millennia before the first hominid?
Have you ever thought about all those years of silence?
I didn't want to hurt her as she stood there waiting.

I wanted to say something that would please her,
but I couldn't tell her she was right. She was not right.
She was neither right nor wrong, neither light
nor dark. She was neither angel nor demon, neither dove

nor asp. She was neither the one who could save me
nor the one who could damn me. She was neither
the pearl nor the meal, neither the fossil nor the fir.
She was neither judge nor gem, neither catechism

nor catacomb, neither breath nor body nor fire nor fear
nor yes nor no. She was neither nil nor love
in this half-life world, neither the bomb, nor the flash,
nor the wave that washes everything away.

Well? she said, nearly spitting, her eyes flaring still.
Which . . . one . . . do . . . you . . . want?
And my answer held there, like a flame,
in the deepening silence between us.

DAN ALBERGOTTI

The Night Nurse Comes

to take his pulse and shut off the alarm,
her pink nails leaving little jaundiced dents in his forearm.

Today he cannot eat or walk or read or speak.
His glazed eyes follow me around the room, and blink.

When I shake the cup of ice, he flicks his gray bird-tongue—
as she commands, under her breath, *You must be the son.*

PATRICK PHILLIPS

Nocturne

Night, in its tide
of coming and going
is a restless
provenance, thinking's
bride. No night can be
absolute: light against it
articulate as pinprick,

fattened as a low-
slung moon. Night is light's
ghost. To know night
is to know what seems
most to have left us,
what sings across
the currents rising.

Even in the dark
we sail through a world
scrimshawed by light.
The lesson of night
is the lesson of how,
within it, grass and lilacs
perfume, crickets treble.

How in it, our breath
becomes an empire,
our bodies, hungry gods.
Dear Night, for all your refusal,
when I open my eyes,
I open them, to their own light.
I know that death is a lie.

MELANIE ALMEDER

Normalization of Deviance

1986, winter of Challenger disaster, O-rings,
solid rocket boosters, southern cold snaps.
Dad blinked at a break in the news coverage,
walked out the door, leaving my brother and me
saying for days, He was right here—
as if the man were a ring of lost keys.

He returned six weeks later, but this scene
repeated into routine. His duffel bag remained
on the hearth, half-filled with Twinkies,
yardage stats on touchdown passes,
newspaper clippings on the sheriff's
helicopter purchases. Always unknown

when he would come and go. My brother and I
were sixteen and ten. Ran the house accordingly.
I'd spit in the stew, forgetting I'd have to eat it, too.
My brother paid me a quarter a day not to cry.
Dad downplayed the returns to a simple Hey,
head nod, stacks of 100s for groceries and heat.

Five years earlier we'd day-tripped to the future:
viewed Space Shuttle Columbia, OV-102 being built.
It loomed over Florida's flatness, sat stiff
and upright like a scared schoolgirl. The metal
scaffolding alongside it, an organized mess
of angles, impressive as the shuttle itself.

I tripped on the newly paved tarmac, still ridged
from no wear. Dad began yelling how he'd sue,
told me it would be the ugliest scar, doom me
to short men who played guitar. His parenting style
was listing off dramatic dangers: poltergeist head-
swivels, lawn-mowered toes, detached retinas.

But my fears were the seemingly harmless: a father
in a white bath robe standing by my bed, a black
government Buick pulling into the drive. So, I wasn't
surprised when the billion-dollar marvel turned to dust
over the Texas sky. A bundle of titanium brought down
by a single cut from a small piece of falling foam.

CHARLOTTE PENCE

Not a Word

I don't remember how or where it started
or which of us to blame—I only know it took
a weekend, midsummer, before the silence broke.
We passed each other in hallways,
our shadows the hue and temper of steel,
and I can still feel the jangle of nerves
like a jailor's keys. Had I flirted with—
or even kissed—another woman? Were you
somehow betraying me? You buried yourself
in classics, Eliot and James, while I loitered
on the porch, trying to judge the angles
of the rain. I kept waiting for you to make
some wry remark, about fools who search
for better lives in books they wish they'd written,
about the diaries and albums people box
in attics—explosives ready to trip.
Instead, I cooked, you washed the dishes;
you drove, I pumped the gas.
We sipped each other's cups of trials,
and made them, in time, our own.
We ambled Asia, Europe, sharing
many points of concord (though fewer
and fewer, after the first hot years,
of contact). Which is to say, we did our best,
and one damp Saturday and Sunday
refused to speak. Had I made a comment
about the comet of gray streaking your hair?
Or maybe you teased me once too often
about my career as an armchair Marxist
and the image I held sacred of my mother
serving the rich at holiday and wedding fêtes—
planting hors d'oeuvres with toothpicks
wrapped in colored plastic, *flags*
of the petty bourgeois. I might have frowned
at your morning breath, or coq au vin,

or coldness toward your father's second wife.
Or it could be (and now I am guessing
wildly) I trotted out some dumb pretension
over drinks with guests—concerning, say,
the *fragrantness* of the wine—and you,
in that polite little way you had, cleared
your throat and noted: *That's not a word.*

GREG FRASER

Note to the Addict Who Robbed Us on a Landscaping Job

—University Heights, Newark, New Jersey

You could have turned to greed, tried to pull out
a lawnmower or tuck weed whackers under each arm.
The leaf blower was a cooler pot of porridge —
shoulder straps, a detachable chute.
We didn't think twice as you zigzagged up the road,
mumbling to some muse. We turned our heads,
and you were wind, just like the machine on your back.

Any black comic will swear a dope fiend can't be caught,
but you trailed an aura-wake — heat streaks woven
across South Orange Avenue, from University
Heights to the projects my mother once rose in.

Know that we could have pursued,
even brought back the power blower (and saved
ourselves) for a fix-worth of bills.
But, rightfully, you would have blown
if our rusty pickup truck came clanking your way.

We left it to the summer's judgment — fearing
our small boss and sour there was likely
a man brown as all of us selling you
something so sick you would risk
stealing from we who carry axes,
stakes and blades for a living.

KYLE DARGAN

Obsessed

I tell my husband I would eat him
if he was already dead and I was starving
on some remote island without Kroger or canned food.
I would eat the dogs, I say, I would eat
my mother, whom I love most in the world.
I'd cut off unessential parts of my flesh
and cake the wounds with mud.
I am smiling when I tell him
I might even eat a stranger.

He says I'm obsessed and he wishes
I would talk about something else.
That's the way it is in marriage.
You want to think your body
isn't a gift, a glass of water on the window sill
drinking its own light. You want to be separate somehow
from the room you live in, the town with its small eyes
and varicose veins.

All day I have almost seen spiders
dart in and out of my periphery.
And finally, tossing greasy turkey parts to the dogs,
a granddaddy long legs
scales the white wall of my corning ware dish,
takes a bit of gizzard in its mouth
and retreats. I had always heard spiders
eat only other bugs, preferably still alive.
My husband tells me he doesn't think
the granddaddy long leg is really a spider.
I hear what I want to hear:
                              none of us
live in our bodies, doing what's expected
of someone with our number of legs.

I am not a daughter, a worker, a wife. I am not from this country.

Though I wear the countenance of a citizen,
my countenance is not edible, and therefore worth less than my body.

My raw, soft body.
Tender body.

MARY CROCKETT HILL

Ode to My Hands

Five-legged pocket spiders, knuckled
starfish, grabbers of forks, why
do I forget that you love me:
your willingness to button my shirts,
tie my shoes—even scratch my head!
which throbs like a traffic jam, each thought
leaning on its horn. I see you

waiting anyplace always
at the ends of my arms—for the doctor,
for the movie to begin, for
freedom—so silent, such
patience! testing the world
with your bold myopia: faithful,
ready to reach out at my
softest suggestion, to fly up
like two birds when I speak, two
brown thrashers brandishing verbs
like twigs in your beaks, lifting
my speech the way pepper springs
the tongue from slumber. O!

If only they knew the unrestrained
innocence of your intentions,
each finger a cappella, singing
a song that rings like rain
before it falls—that never falls!
Such harmony: the bass thumb, the
pinkie's soprano, the three tenors
in between: kind quintet x 2
rowing my heart like a little boat
upon whose wooden seat I sit
strummed by Sorrow. Or maybe

I misread you completely
and you are dreaming a tangerine, one
particular hot tamale, a fabulous
banana! to peel suggestively,
like thigh-high stockings: grinning
as only hands can grin
down the legs—caramel, cocoa,
black-bean black, vanilla—such lubricious
dimensions, such public secrets!
Women sailing the streets

with God's breath at their backs.
Think of it! No!
Yes: let my brain sweat, make my
veins whimper: without you, my five-hearted
fiends, my five-headed hydras, what
of my mischievous history? The possibilities
suddenly impossible—feelings
not felt, rememberings un-
remembered—all the touches
untouched: the gallant strain

of a pilfered ant, tiny muscles
flexed with fight, the gritty
sidewalk slapped after a slip, the pulled
weed, the plucked flower—a buttercup!
held beneath Dawn's chin—the purest kiss,
the caught grasshopper's kick, honey,
chalk, charcoal, the solos teased
from guitar. Once, I played
viola for a year and never stopped

to thank you—my two angry sisters,
my two hungry men—but you knew
I just wanted to know
what the strings would say
concerning my soul, my whelming
solipsism: this perpetual solstice

where one + one = everything
and two hands teach a dawdler
the palpable alchemy
of an unreasonable world.

TIM SEIBLES

Ode to Silence

Glory to the half rest, to the breath
        between the third and fourth beats,
                the dwindling arrow of the decrescendo,

to the sunrise over Malibu, and its sleeping
        starlets, the empty horizon,
                the city's great thought still looming,

to parked cars, the cold engine seconds before
        ignition dreaming of the road
                unwound and endless,

to the lull before ecstasy, the saint's vigil
        of the dark soul in suffering,
                the grip of the heart before release,

to the inaction of love before the reaction,
        of the hand before it reaches out,
                its sharp twitch of self-consciousness,

to the embryo, the soft dream of the
        womb, the golden truth of genesis,
                the sustained hush and its amplitude.

MEGAN SEXTON

Of Thorns

Go down our potholed road, past the last light in the last house
and the old glass foundry now slated for demolition, go past
the tattered heaps of salted snow, the tracks, a cold sun sliding
like an egg yolk off a plate and over the cross-tied edge
of the world, and you will come to where the creek, in flood,
scrapes a rut through gravel, but it shouldn't be a problem,
not this time of year, and finally the road just peters out
into a deer track and then not even that—just hills, just Arkansas—
and it's not pretty, not anybody's pastoral dream, only scrub
and broken bottles, and that rusted pipe through which,
improbably, a dogwood has found the light, and there's no shepherd
stepping from the trees with his crook, not even the curve of moon
that gathers each night its flock of polished stones, but down there
in that shabby closeness, that's where whatever it is that saves me is,
where, praise be to something, it waits in briars like Jesus or literature.

DAVIS MCCOMBS

On New Year's Eve

we make midnight a maquette of the year:
frostlight glinting off snow to solemnize
            the vows we offer to ourselves in near
silence: the competition shimmerwise

of champagne and chandeliers to attract
laughter and cheers: the glow from the fireplace
            reflecting the burning intra-red pact
between beloveds: we cosset the space

of a fey hour, anxious gods molding our
hoped-for adams with this temporal clay:
            each of us edacious for shining or
rash enough to think sacrifice will stay

this fugacious time: while stillness suspends
vitality in balance, as passions
            struggle with passions for sway, the mind wends
towards what's to come: a callithump of fashions,

ersatz smiles, crowded days: a bloodless cut
that severs soul from bone: a long aching
            quiet in which we will hear nothing but
the clean crack of our promises breaking.

EVIE SHOCKLEY

On Speaking with an Old Schoolmate after His Physics Lecture at a Local University

Despite the intent behind the broom handle,
spokes ticking off the bicycle wheel
like milliseconds from an atomic clock,
the yellow hyphens in the center of the road
linking constants and inertia,
compliance of steel and rubber and asphalt,
friction of skin and bone: how matter vibrates,
compresses, splinters for one common end,
leaving its signature in broken trajectories of light
across a caved-in windshield,
you said you only remembered
a cat's-eye marble rolling slowly toward your cheek,
green swirl corkscrewing from the glass orb
and unraveling across the curb
where you landed. "Kids," you chuckled,
and in those words you forgave us again
just as you always did our transgressions
of loogies and wedgies,
green-pinecone-and-dog-shit bombs.
After the stainless pins, the cast
with your preacher's and parents'
wishes scrawled across it,
the grafts from the small of your back,
the exercises with pinto-bean cans,
you traded us your Mickey Mantles,
encased as if rare specimens defying entropy,
for our abused Niekros and Fisks.
After our "you're all right for a geek,"
after you had turned your back to us,
cradling your atrophied arm at your chest,

we pelted you with the apples
our mothers had packed so lovingly for us.

ADAM VINES

On the Wood Storks

Behind the movie theater's neon *beau monde*
cooled the dank waters of a retention pond,

cyclone-fenced, palm-guarded, overgrown.
You walked there when you wanted to be alone.

For weeks nothing stirred the blackened reeds,
which were enough, those days you felt in need.

Then, one evening, through the gathered gloom,
as if something uncanny had entered a room,

across algae green as an Alpine meadow,
eight white ghosts floated faintly through the shadow,

pausing, worrying, then slowly moving on,
the waters like a chessboard scattered with white pawns.

When bankers review their fat portfolios,
they draw such dark beaks open and closed,

great shears to cut some invisible thread.
The pale birds stalked like something newly dead.

One lifted a black-edged wing, in search of food,
and somehow that broke your somber mood.

Yet on they marched, like Dante's souls through Hell,
awaiting the Last Judgment's redeeming bell,

working their way in silence, fallen aristocrats.
You said they looked like ladies' hats,

white as the color of love, if love has color—
bright white, you meant, only a little duller.

WILLIAM LOGAN

Origami

The kids are good at this. Their nimble fingers
Double and fold and double fold the pages,
Making mimetic icons for all ages.
The floor of the school is littered with dead ringers:

Songbirds that really flap their wings, rare cranes,
Bleached bonsai trees, pale ghouls, two kinds of hats,
Dwarf stars, white roses, Persian copycats,
Small packet boats, whole fleets of flyable planes.

Some of the girls, some of the older ones,
Make effigies of boys and . . . "Goodness sakes!"
They ask what I can make. "I make mistakes."
"No really, Mr. Greg!" They don't like puns.

I tear out a page and say, "I've made a bed."
They frown at me. I'll have to lie on it.
"See, it's a sheet." But they're not buying it,
And seem to imply ("You crazy!") it's all in my head.

I head for home, where even more white lies
Take shape. The page is a window filled with frost,
An unformed thought, a thought I had, but lost.
The page is the sclera of someone rolling his eyes

As it becomes (you'll recognize the trick)
Tomorrow morning, laundry on the line,
The South Pole, circa 1929,
The mainsail of the *Pequod*, Moby Dick,

The desert sand, the shore, the arctic waste
Of untold tales, where hero and author together
Must turn, out of the silence, into the whether-
Or-not-they-find-the-grail. Not to your taste?

The page is a flag of surrender. I surrender—
To the rustle of programs before a serious talk,
The sound of seashells, seas, the taste of chalk,
The ghost of snow, the ghost of the sky in December,

And frozen surfaces of ponds, which hide
Some frigid stirring, something. (What have I done?)
It's the napkin at a table set for one,
The shade drawn in a room where someone died.

The pages keep on turning. They assume
More shapes than I can put my finger on,
A wall of silence, curtains, doors, false dawn,
The stared-at ceiling of my rented room.

"You crazy, Mr. Greg." The voices call;
The sheet on the unmade bed is gone awry.
I sit at my little desk in mid-July
Throwing snowballs at the Sheetrock wall.

GREG WILLIAMSON

Outside Winn Dixie in Suburban Plaza

Late Saturday night, 1986, and again I had no one
to hang out with, just a few poems
and a notion of what to do, when I saw a girl
not much older than sixteen in the back of a car
under the drunken parking lot lights,
her eyes watered-down with a slacked milky glaze,
full of what I knew must be her childhood
being pushed off a north Georgia cliff by two boys
running into Winn Dixie for more PBR.

After more than twenty years, I like to think I've helped
enough people along the way to quiet my regret,
repaired the heavy elegy I carry on my back
for my father and what he might say,
"Never leave a stranger stranded."

As I walk through my house, I check the locks
on each door, turn off the lights, the t.v., the gas logs,
then up stairs to the hall and around a pile of Legos
left on the floor. I step lightly to each child's room,
place a train on the dresser, adjust the bed covers,
tuck a bear under an arm, turn off a closet light.
Each cheek is dry to my kiss. Room to room,
I make my rounds like a doctor or maybe like Superman
spinning the earth backwards to save Lois Lane.

WILLIAM WALSH

Palestine, Texas

"I've never been," I said to my friend who'd just come back from there. "Oh you should definitely go," she said. "The original Palestine is in Illinois." She went on, "A pastor was driven out by Palestine's people and it hurt him so badly he had to rename somewhere else after it. Or maybe it goes back to a 17th century Frenchman who traveled with his vision of milk and honey, or the nut who believed in dual seeding." "What's that?" I asked. "That's when an egg is fertilized by two sperm," she said. "Is that even viable?" I asked. "It is," she said, "on rare occasions, though nothing guarantees the longevity of the resulting twins." She spoke like a scientist but was a professor of the humanities at heart. "Viability," she added, "depends on the critical degree of disproportionate defect distribution for a miracle to occur. If there is life, only one twin lives." That night we went to the movies looking for a good laugh. It was a Coen Brothers feature whose unheralded opening scene rattled off Palestine this, Palestine that and the other, it did the trick. We were granted the right to exist. It must have been there and then that my wallet slipped out of my jeans' back pocket and under the seat. The next morning, I went back. With a flashlight that the manager had lent me I found the wallet unmoved. This was the second time in a year that I'd lost and retrieved this modern cause of sciatica in men. Months earlier it was at a lily pond I'd gone hiking to with the same previously mentioned friend. It was around twilight. Another woman, going in with her boyfriend as we were coming out, picked it up, put it in her little backpack, and weeks later texted me the photo of his kneeling and her standing with right hand over mouth, to thwart the small bird in her throat from bursting. If the bird escapes, the cord is severed, and the heart plummets. She didn't want the sight of joy caught in her teeth. He sat his phone camera on its pod and set it in lapse mode, she wrote in her text to me. I welled up. She would become a bride and my wallet was part of the proposal. This made me a token of their bliss, though I'm not sure how her fiancé might feel about my intrusion, if he would care at all. "It's a special wallet," I texted back. "It's been with me for the better part of two decades ever since a good friend got it for me as a present." "He was from Ohio," I turned and said to my film mate who was listening to my story. "Ohio?" She seemed surprised. "Yes," I replied quizzically. "There's also a Palestine in Ohio," she said. "Barely anyone lives there anymore. All of them barely towns off country roads."

FADY JOUDAH

Pfc. Mason Buxton Embraces the Suck

Back home in the Louisiana night, my wife
squeezes the hand of some ponytailed nurse,
cursing my name with every push
while I wake again in the cradle
of fucking civilization, another day
the same, decked out in battle rattle,
lugging an idiot stick, extra mags
stuffed in my flak jacket, roam
the same brown streets and wait
for necktied Beltway clerks
to sort out this Sunni and Shiite shit—
and I can almost hear her grunts and groans
and the crunch of ice between her teeth,
almost see her lips wrenching with pain
as the doctor inserts the forceps into her
and tells her, *Again*, and, *One more*, and she screams—
and from a hundred feet I feel the blast
behind me and tuck beneath the rain
of dirt and rock, then sidle along a wall
and turkey peek around the corner,
see vics spread-eagled on the ground,
some dead, some dying eyes-wide-open
in the arms of women already wearing black,
and at the checkpoint, a pool of blood
and fur, a donkey ear (*Shock and
hee-haw*, we call it later), then I'm holding
a soldier whose arm hangs from his shoulder
by shreds of sinew and skin.
A month goes by, and I'm at Ft. Living Room.
I have a daughter and lie awake in bed,
sleepless at oh three hundred,
seeing behind my eyes the placid sun
hung like a medal in the bone-colored sky.

BRENT NEWSOM

Phone Sex

is not the subject of this poem.
I wrote that at the top so you
would start to read, thinking you
would be a little hurt at first,
but then get interested in what
I have to say about the Issues,
like Art and Love. Most likely Death.
I hope you don't feel tricked, but please
don't scan your eyes along these lines
in hopes that phone sex will recur.
Don't look for heavy breathing here.
Don't think about what the hand,
the other one that doesn't hold
the phone, is doing. There's just no way
I'm going to write about the voice
that whispers some scenario—
some fantasy about a hammock,
a girl with Angelina lips
and a pitcher of iced lemonade
from which she's just removed a cube
and drawn it slowly like a balm
into her ruby mouth as she
approaches you. Reader, put
that notion right out of your head.
Frankly, it's embarrassing.
I'm talking about Art, or Death,
so listen. I'll describe it. Stay
on the line. I'm almost there.

JULIANA GRAY

Pocketknives

Carried like time, consulted
as often when the sermon
droned on past noon, hay bailer
broke a chain, any other
lingering moments their scarred
and calloused workflesh idled,
the blades pried free the way wives
might slip a ribbon, that same
delicate tug when forge-craft
sharpened what light sun or bulb
provided as they trimmed dirt
from the undersides of nails,
surfaced splinters, bled blisters,
a tool but more than a tool
each time they rasped a whetstone
across steel until it flashed
pure as silver, then a rag
doused in oil to rub new-bright
the handles hewed from antler,
pearl, hardwood and ivory
laced with brass or gold, the one
vanity of men caught once
when dead in a coat and tie,
so ordered from catalogs,
saved and traded for, searched for
in sheds and fields if lost, passed
father to son as heirlooms,
like talismans carried close
though most times, cloaked as the hearts
of these men who rarely spoke
their fears and hopes, let their words
clench inside a locked silence.

RON RASH

Poem

for Brigit Pegeen Kelly

In this town I still say I'm from, one night
two boys played catch with a cat, a black cat.
They were the kind of boys who sewed eagles
to the backs of their denim jackets and smoked
a resinous weed with the density of a star.

It was difficult to see this cat near the end
of the dock where dark lake water caught
the cat each time they threw it in the air
and into the lake with its fuel and oil slicks
now invisible but palpable, most likely,
to the cat.
              And it's truer to say they were
playing catch with the lake, because the lake
gave the cat right back to them each time,
exactly where they waited.
                            The cat was easier
to see in the water, oddly enough, than it was
in the air. A light above the fuel station
at the end of the dock glinted on its wet fur,
you see.
          Otherwise you wouldn't have known
it was there, for it made no sound while it swam,
only screamed when it sailed out over the water
and into the water, where it then went silent,
a shadow swimming in a larger shadow.

This enraged the boys, who took it as an affront
that the cat did not complain, so they threw it
farther and higher each time, and each time
the cat came back, trying to find a place where
the boys were not. There was no place like that.

It might have looked as if the boys guided

the cat back to shore, as if indeed the cat meant
to get back to them.
                                It wanted to get back
somewhere, a box in a basement
next to a humming furnace, most likely.

It's fair to ask why no one stopped this.
After all, I did punch one of the boys
in the face and knock him out.
                                That was before
the cat, though. The timing was wrong, as much
as we'd like to believe he got his punishment
before his crime. Also, there were two of them,
one to bend down and retrieve the cat and one
to keep me away. They were bigger by then.

They may not have stopped growing, in fact.
They are giants. One of them now paints bridges.
I wish I could say a pharaoh commissioned
his work to commemorate a stone causeway
over the lower Nile, that along the bridge's span
in subtle variations he painted the fine profiles
of cats in their eternal stillnesses.
                                Instead, he hangs
by a harness over the highway and covers the sides
of each bridge with green paint. He makes
a good deal of money but little sound dangling there
above traffic.
                    He has shaved his head, now grown
more pointed and delicate from hours in the sun,
perhaps, or from the way we begin here to picture
him transformed into the image of the creature
he has certainly forgotten.
                                You might even say
he has come to resemble, in profile himself against
the bridge in sunset light, a fine-boned pharaoh,
his skin tawny as he awaits eternity, his ears
sharp and laid back this evening, away from

his family and dangling from the overpass.

                                    He turns
now in the harness to watch the sun descend
to a horizon shimmering in the heat like water.

He knows it is only corn out there, but in spite
of himself he sees only a vast green lake.
As when a river still flows in a flooded valley under
the greater body of water,

                        so do the cars below him.
Perhaps just now he remembers the cat, which swam
under the dock but did not appear on the other side.

PAUL BONE

Poem Found

—New Orleans, September 2005

. . . and God said, "Let there be a dome in the midst
of the waters" and into the dome God put

the poor, the addicts, the blind, and the oppressed.
God put the unsightly sick and the crying young

into the dome and the dry land did not appear.
And God allowed those who favored themselves

born in God's image to take dominion over
the dome and everything that creeped within it

and made them to walk to and fro above it
in their jumbo planes and in their copy rooms

and in their conference halls. And then
God brooded over the dome and its multitudes

and God saw God's own likeness in the shattered
tiles and the sweltering heat and the polluted rain.

God saw everything and chose to make it very good.
God held the dome up to the light

like an open locket and in every manner called
the others to look inside and those who saw

rested on that day and those who didn't
went to and fro and walked up and down

the marsh until the loosened silt gave way
to a void, and darkness covered the faces with deep sleep.

MARTHA SERPAS

Portrait of My Ex as the Letter X

At first you think it marks the spot: on texts
hand-inked on rolls of calfskin, mapping treks
to sites of opulent and tragic shipwrecks,
the legendary treasure of the Aztecs.
Then those same black lines shift in context.
A rating promises the kind of sex
they don't allow in the local multiplex.
In triplicate it flashes, calls and becks
to a lawyer with a desperate yen for latex
who, later, cleans his glasses and inspects
the document you've not signed, but hexed
with that same slashing mark, the intellect's
dilemma, the heart's unrelenting vortex,
the blank you'll never solve for: exactly X.

JULIANA GRAY

A Preacher Who Takes Up Serpents Laments the Presence of Skeptics in His Church

Every Sabbath they come,
gawk like I'm something
in a tent at a county fair.
In the vanity of their unbelief
they will cover an eye with a camera
and believe it will make them see.
They see nothing. I show them Mark 16
but they believe in the word of man.
They believe death is an end.

And would live like maggots,
wallow in the filth of man's creation.
Less than a mile from here
the stench of sulphur rises
like fog off the Pigeon River.
They do not believe it a sign
of their own wickedness.
They cannot see a river
is a vein in God's arm.

When I open the wire cages
they back away like crayfish
and tell each other I am insane—
terrified I may not be.
Others, my own people, whisper
He tempts God, and will not join me.
They cannot understand surrender
is humility, not arrogance,
that a man afraid to die cannot live.

Only the serpents sense the truth.
The diamondback's blunted tail is silent,
the moccasin's pearl-white mouth closed.
The coral snake coils around
my wrist, a harmless bright bracelet,
in the presence of the Lord.

RON RASH

Preparing the Tongue

In my hands, it's cold and knowing
as bone. I unwind its gauze, mummy-like,
rub my wrist blue against the cactus
of its buds. Were it still cradled inside
the clammy cow mouth, I should want
to enchant it: let it taste the oil in my skin,
lick the lash of my eye. What I do instead
is lacerate the frozen muscle, tear
the brick-thick cud conductor in half to fit
a ceramic red pot. Its cry reaches me
from some heap of butchered heads as I hack
away like an axe murderer. I choke down
the stink of its heated moo, make carnage
of my own mouth, add garlic.

LAURIE ANN GUERRERO

Primitive Baptist

Aunt Ethel went to the foot washing church. The Primitive Baptists
　　　did the things they did on the other side of town
in a brick building that could use a new roof. I only had it
　　　secondhand what went on behind those weather-rawed
　　　doors—no speaking in tongues
where my parents and I attended at the worldly and sophisticated
　　　First Baptist Church. Our preacher had been to a college,
and there was air-conditioning and carpet down the aisles, an
　　　organ to mend our singing. The amen-ing had a self-aware
　　　quality. One of the deacons
owned a roofing company, and we all would have been mortified
　　　to be caught splashing tap water over a neighbor's
　　　bunioned feet.

I have a friend who is modern in every respect, but when she's
　　　between errands, unable to see the point in any of it,
　　　she'll hear herself praying
that the Second Coming come now, the haze-grayed skies torn.
　　　open, Gabriel's horn to blow. And when the clouds keep
　　　stubbornly shut, what else is there
but to hold the car in the road aimed into the next curve, as
　　　determined as the Primitive Baptists emerging onto the
　　　steps after service,
fully shod, the fat Windsor knots of the men's ties snugged into
　　　the collars of their short-sleeved dress shirts, women in
　　　shapeless cotton shifts
faded from too many afternoons line dried and wind snapped, no
　　　pantyhose since they knew there was going to be a foot
　　　washing. Who wouldn't want to feel

just that pure? They still glowed with it as they went to yank open
　　　the doors of high-mileage sedans and short bed pickups
　　　that would be
leaning on the same low tire outside the Brown Shoe factory come
　　　Monday. There's a trick to opening your heart. Most of

what's in there can't get out fast enough, but deep down
you'll come across some fleck of spirit that won't be washed away
        or made humble though it might soften and shine a bit as
        you bend
to bathe someone's feet in a dented metal basin and sit still for the
        same to be done unto you, then, hands dried, reshod, you
        can't stop hearing
the hymn of commitment across the unpaved parking lot, each step
        pressing a breath of dust from the gravel burnished amber
        in the evening's unstirred light.

BOBBY ROGERS

The Professor and Mary Ann

On her the smile of a rag doll readies
for flattery or purpose because corn
is her origin, corn her choice,
as if she split the life of a woman
and traded the hips and breathy sex
of an actress for cutoffs, a tablecloth
halter top, and a name rustic as Norma
Jean. And he is nameless, a guy in white
with eyes like a microscope
and his face flush to the lens of escape,
too distracted or dumb to fall swinish
to the spell of a pout or hair like flame.

In his dream he mends the radio diodes,
irrigates beach sand, jars a new species
of *Thorybes confusis*, and repairs the Minnow
with the gum of an undiscovered phylum
of mammalian plant. And when they gather
in Sweden, those of science and judgement,
he will have charted the uncharted desert isle,
and the world will know his name.

In her dream she is Ginger,
glitter flaring its gown at her fullness
as she walks the voodoo island walk.
In her dream the howl of millions rises,
the jaw of the skipper drops, the jungle eyes
of the first mate bulge into the monkeyhood,
and the mind of whitest science
drops its squint from the small crisis
of extinction and follows her as dawn
wells into the lagoon's mouth.

AUSTIN HUMMELL

The Progress of Night

In the late elegiac light insects
      chide the frail contraption of the sky,
            its faulty system of pulleys and wires.

Piteous stars circuit the stripped gears
      of galaxy as crickets keep grinding
            out twilight's tinny, dwindling music.

Again that pale immigrant blunders in
      to watch over the progress of night,
            to observe the grim magics we practice,

all the oaths we take and make and utter.
      What comfort can we offer another
            traveler under this same unsteady scaffold?

We'll find no charm against calamity.
      Though the dark architecture of the heart
            is buttressed by sternum, girded by ribs,

we build our lives from its very trembling.

AMY FLEURY

Rahab

The boys came to my house
on the edge of Prattville
and asked if I could love them
and I said I reckon I can
if you take off your shoes
and put them by the mat
and choose which one of you
goes first because no matter
what you heard I'm not like that.
They were from ten miles
or more away and had been
walking through the woods.
First I washed the first one's
feet and rubbed him
with Astrolube. Then Elroy,
who is the Sheriff, knocked
on the door and I opened
the door and he said, Bring out
them boys you got in there.
I said, Yes, I saw them
walk to the store and I saw them
talk to Aunt Evie and that's
the last I saw them.
You better hurry if you aim
to catch them. See I had
hidden them under the stairs
with the canned peaches
and coats. You better hurry,
I told Elroy. Then the boys
returned from under the stairs
and I said, Now swear
you won't kill me or my family
and they swore it.
They put on their shoes
and coats and the first one

stayed in the doorway.
Rahab, he said. Rabbit.
I'm coming back for you.
When the time came,
I hung my lingerie
in the window and said
my prayers. I haven't seen them
since. All my neighbors are dead.

JILLIAN WEISE

Re: Liability

: our concern addressed to Mendel Grossman, 1941

Light, white enough to take over. Imperial light. Erasing hairlines,
an ear, the edge of teeth, the edge of skin, the edge of skin to skin,
sky. The film's large grain, summoned into bodies by the dim
eye of your permitted camera, now unauthorized. But this is not
ekphrasis: They called you the statistics man, the record keeper;
you were made to shoot mugshots for I.D.'s. Did they think in
the after-hour you'd go blind? Instead, the breadmaker's stooped
shoulders. Toddlers running to the gate. Women, aging. You were
shameless. The camera they gave you, hidden under your long
coat. The coat, opened enough, click. The everyday ghetto, carts
and shovels, now shadows, now movement, blurred. Each night,
you returned the day's negatives to the dark, your nails brown and
brittle from midnight chemicals. You did not sleep. At dawn—the
shutter, release. Isn't this Bresson's *decisive moment?* The exit that
opens when one person looks another in the eye? When you dressed
in the dank morning, bringing the camera strap around, securing
the machine to your chest like a bomb, what did you know? That
you had to? I never had to do anything. Would I know it, if I did?

REBECCA GAYLE HOWELL

The Ring

These days, you don't just buy a solitaire.
You look for flaws with magnifying loupes,
check color grades, make setting choices: flared
four-prong cathedral, ridged contour, or flutes
of baguette accents down the sides. The bands,
once standard 14k gold, now come
in weapons-grade titanium. It stands
to reason, one would think, as rings become
unbreakable, the bonds they represent
might, too. But every master jeweler knows
about the unseen structural punishment
gems undergo, the blades, the saws, the blows
received on every face, the grinding hours
it takes for shapes like teardrops, hearts, and flowers.

CARRIE JERRELL

River of Mirrors

The long sleek bass
   bearded by the current
lays in the running
   home the river is

and the river washes over
   the fish and the force
helps to steady it
   as it wavers slightly

still floating in place
   in the rush of current
near a large stone jutting
   up into the air where

a white sycamore branch
   leans down gently
and among all the infinite
   simultaneous details

of the world this one is
   one too many to hold
suddenly and the idea
   of god always suffers

and things fall apart and
   moving very slightly
oblivious in its way
   soon the fish is going

to be dragged out of
   this habitat of speed
and rushing water that is
   its wild green home

and be dashed against
    the stone where leaves
of the sycamore curl
    and someone with a line

in the water feels the pull
    of something hidden
leap suddenly flashing
    like a mirror in the sun.

STEVE SCAFIDI

Ruin

There is no antecedent. There was God
and there was the sea. To hear us tell it,
there was an earth built for us. But listen—
For a long, long time, there was nothing
but God and the wine-black sea. His voice
against Her waters. Always.

Don't you know what it's like
to love in the dark? The way the beloved
moves in sleep against you—
reaching for hip or hands?
A body can love another body through proximity
alone. For the beloved,

someone could be convinced to
build anything. Someone could be
talked into making a thing like light.
Firmament. I could see Him giving the earth
its bounty and the sea crying out:
I need you inside me. I need to carry you inside me.
God would reach down and give Himself to Her,
and She would smile, rub Her belly,
say: *Look, my beloved. Look what we have made.*

For a time, they must have been quite happy.

TJ JARRETT

Sandhill Crane

A wineskin sloshing on stilts, you decant
a nauseous honk. Your eyes are beads of honey,
gray feathers watered down in weak coffee.
Why cock your scarlet head? What you want

rarely emerges from frost, and no worm
wriggles in this upturned earth. Straight-legged,
you wait, watch morning unshell from its egg.
Hive-minded drone of this weathered swarm,

what you excavate is yours—speckled frog,
serpent's cursive *S*. Ground allows you these
dissections, frantic aerator beak-deep
in black loam. Soon, ghost, swath of living fog,

this will green and you'll be gone. Forgive
the prairie's subtlety—like nothing else alive.

ERIC SMITH

Scale

At the base of a mountain,
you are small, and the world
clicks smoothly over you.

At the base of a mountain,
you glow inside *almost*,
and few lights are so generous.

At the base of a mountain,
death is inevitable. Look
how the rock has swallowed
centuries. You could melt
into its sun-ovened roughness.

At the base of a mountain,
you see, in the hazeless light,
the revised version of yourself.
You think, I will do what it takes
to breathe this prickling air.
You think, I will turn alarm bells
into pine needles, and then
I'll walk over them. You think,
I'll let my hair grow again.
I'll eat apples, avocados.

You think, there is nothing
ahead and nothing behind.
You think of a thousand songs
and choose silence. It whistles
softly to you. No. It's whistling
to the mountain. It doesn't
even know you're there.

CATHERINE PIERCE

Sea Glass for a Second Son

How much can a person take
secondhand? Having come first,
I never made do with hand-me-downs,
but you—I worry you have little else;
so I'm out for sea glass this morning
with fog and herons because the tide
is low and time left short and because
you love it, each beached chip
another for the shoebox full of mostly green,
occasionally brown, rarely blue
shards the sea has tumbled smooth
and harmless. By the time I finish
the mile north to mudflats and turn back
to breakfast with you, by now awake, it sounds
in my pocket nothing like coins or anything else
so worthless to someone who'll give
more than Manhattan for a handful.

STEPHEN CUSHMAN

Sea Psalm

We see no ships at harbor. The sea is the sky's

gray mirror, and I am
                in the dream of its plain reflection, the still water

      before a wave's ascent.

       What rise left in me   is left to follow you to shore.
Is an edge to narrow

what shoulders you—I cut the beach
                to bring you to water—

      and the odd wonder

you shoulder,   like a one-winged bird.

I want to call you *love*, as I want
            to call the driftwood *house*.   Daily,

we age into erosion's remnants,
              carving our lines

out of the coast, and I am learning to forgive
             my longing to make strangeness

unstrange;   that our shadows, subsuming us,

do not complete us.
              Where in the shell-mottled sand

will we make our ragged bed?   Now, *love*,

      the sea-wind salts our young skin,

our bodies turn to shell:

     let us be emptied
          as this off-season shore,

     to be loved
for what we lack.

JENNIFER CHANG

Self-Checkout

The paradox of choice: supply demands
variety, but just how many brands
of waffles does a woman need to test
before selecting one that suits her best?
From waffles on to syrup (which entails
the nuances of sausage links, and sales),
it's awful. Though Wynona hopes to build
her option-tolerance, last week she killed
a morning, slack-jawed, at the hardware store
trying to pick the perfect two-by-four-
inch strip of cardstock (teal a tad too jade,
luna too mucus, golf course lacking glade,
only to find her subtle English pea,
wall-sized, was not so subtle). You can see
why after several minutes making faces
at her reflection in the freezer cases
this afternoon, she simply calls it quits—
to hell with waffles, butter, bacon bits—
and drops her basket in the sea of feet
like a bomb or baby. Sure, she needs to eat,
would maybe call for takeout could she spin
the order without going in again.
As for delivery, it sounds terrific
prior to toppings ("Ma'am, please be specific,
which kind of crust?"), and drive-through joints divide
their menu into menus: pick a side,
pick three, in fact. No thank you, that's alright,
Wynona says. She's lost her appetite,
flat dithered out. So—barely getting by—
why won't she make a move to simplify?
She'd like to think that if she had her druthers
she'd ditch the druthers. Not so: like the others
who stand, eyes glazing over, and assay
the stock, Wynona hates to look away,

believes if she could memorize the list
she'd know there's nothing more than this she missed.

CAKI WILKINSON

Self-Portrait as Slinky

It's true I wanted
     to be beautiful before
          authentic. Say the word
               exotic. Say minority—

a coiled, dark curl
     a finger might wrap
          itself in. The long
               staircase, and I was

the momentum
     of metal springs
          descending down
               and down,
a tension

—the long staircase,
     and I was a stacked series
          of spheres finger-tipped
               again into motion,

taut, like a child
     who must please
          the elders and doesn't
               know how, a curl pulled

thin. I wanted to be
     a reckoning, to tornado
          into each day's hard
               hands, that wanton

lurching forward
     in the dark, another
          soaked black ringlet,
               that sudden halting—

TARFIA FAIZULLAH

Shetland

Shorty, lone grazer of Granddaddy's pasture,
brawny, bristle-maned chestnut stuffed with clover,

our horse: intractable, brutish, and mean.
But once, when I was about eight or nine,

I found him idle by the barbwire fence,
just staring—calm, inert—toward the house,

and got a wild hair, thought, I'll stroke his muzzle.
Sidling up, whispering, I put palm to skull—

an anvil; an iron hull shrink-wrapped in hide—
and his story traveled up my arm. This cloud

of sweat and flies and moist, long-rifled breathing,
this piss-hot leathery stink, had being.

I was resolved to spend all day with Shorty,
worried it'd be the only time he'd let me.

He was a rough beast, I a skittish child.
But for once, now, we two were reconciled

and my brain forged for us an island north,
hardships braved, friendships kept, galloping forth.

A rousing age that passed in half an hour.
I heard through the screen door a radio stir,

crackle, and settle on the local news,
wandered away in dew-soaked tennis shoes.

NICK NORWOOD

Signs, Oakvale, Mississippi, 1941

The first time she leaves home is with a man.
On Highway 49, heading north, she watches
the pine woods roll by, and counts on one hand
dead possum along the road, crows in splotches
of light — she knows to watch the signs for luck.
He has a fine car, she thinks. *And money green
enough to buy a dream* — more than she could tuck
under the mattress, in a Bible, or fold between
her powdered breasts. He'd promised land to farm
back home, new dresses, a house where she'd be
queen. (*Was the gap in his teeth cause for alarm?*)
The cards said go. She could roam the Delta, see
things she'd never seen. Outside her window,
nothing but cotton and road signs — stop or slow.

NATASHA TRETHEWEY

Silence

It is not the sand or receding tide,
heavy with salt, that I am thinking of,
my hands rubbing my eyes
as if they were some genie's lamp—
my wishes with me all along. No,
I am thinking of rain at the end of winter—
what a comfort it is
to find hope in the hopeless—
like repetition, like ice.
I am thinking of the cardinal
who tries to fly through that just-cleaned window,
how good it must feel to finally forget,
resting your head on the cool cement.
I am thinking of Cassandra,
whose story's so tragic, it could only have come
from a guilty heart.
I am thinking of silence, the silence I hear
when your name is a question,
your absence somehow making this room
quieter than ever before.

TERRY KENNEDY

Silence

Silence has its own notation: dark
Jottings of duration, but not pitch,
A long black box, or little feathered hitch
Like a new Greek letter or diacritical mark.
Silence is a function of Time, the lark
In flight but not in song. A nothing which
Keeps secrets or confesses. Pregnant, rich,
Or awkward, cold, the pause that makes us hark,
The space before or after: it's the room
In which melody moves, the medium
Through which thought travels, it is golden, best,
Welcome relief to talk-worn tedium.
Before the word itself, it was the womb.
It has a measure. Music calls it rest.

A. E. STALLINGS

Sinners Welcome

I opened up my shirt to show this man
the flaming heart he lit in me, and I was scooped up
like a lamb and carried to the dim warm.
I who should have been kneeling
was knelt to by one whose face
should be emblazoned on every coin and diadem:

no bare-chested boy, but Ulysses
with arms thick from the hard-hauled ropes.
He'd sailed past then clay gods
and the singing girls who might have made of him

a swine. That the world could arrive at me
with him in it, after so much longing—
impossible. He enters me and joy
sprouts from us as from a split seed.

MARY KARR

Sitting Down to Breakfast Alone

Brachest, she called it, gentling grease
over blanching yolks with an expertise
honed from three decades of dawns
at the Longhorn Diner in Loraine,
where even the oldest in the old men's booth
swore as if it were scripture truth
they'd never had a breakfast better,
rapping a glass sharply to get her
attention when it went sorrowing
so far into some simple thing—
the jangly door or a crusted pan,
the wall clock's black, hitchy hands—
that she would startle, blink, then grin
as if discovering them all again.
Who remembers now when one died
the space that he had occupied
went unfilled for a day, then two, three,
until she unceremoniously
plunked plates down in the wrong places
and stared their wronged faces
back to banter she could hardly follow.
Unmarried, childless, homely, "slow,"
she knew coffee cut with chamomile
kept the grocer Paul's ulcer cool,
yarrow in gravy eased the islands
of lesions in Larry Borwick's hands,
and when some nightlong nameless urgency
sent him seeking human company
Brother Tom needed hash-browns with cheese.
She knew to nod at the litany of cities
the big-rig long-haulers bragged her past,
to laugh when the hunters asked
if she'd pray for them or for the quail
they went laughing off to kill,
and then—envisioning one

rising so fast it seemed the sun
tugged at it—to do exactly that.
Who remembers where they all sat:
crook-backed builders, drought-faced farmers,
VF'ers muttering through their wars,
night-shift roughnecks so caked in black
it seemed they made their way back
every morning from the dead.
Who remembers one word they said?
The Longhorn Diner's long torn down,
the gin and feedlots gone, the town
itself now nothing but a name
at which some bored boy has taken aim,
every letter light-pierced and partial.
Sister, Aunt Sissy, Bera Thrailkill,
I picture you one dime-bright dawn
grown even brighter now for being gone
bustling amid the Formica and chrome
of that small house we both called home
during the spring that was your last.
All stories stop: once more you're lost
in something I can merely see:
steam spiriting out of black coffee,
the scorched pores of toast, a bowl
of apple butter like edible soil,
bald cloth, knifelight, the lip of a glass,
my plate's gleaming, teeming emptiness.

CHRISTIAN WIMAN

Skinned

There are, after all, several ways to skin anything. My
    grandmother knew
most of those ways. She had been skinned herself (so to speak)
in that her skin was so often examined and found wanting.
What would one want to do with it, really? Despite the constant
    oiling
which left her arms soft as anyone could possibly desire,
her hands were ruins. She never hit me with them.
My grandfather took her with her hands at her sides.
Laundry water, cotton bolls, horse hide, the blood of goats.
She had to cook and I had to eat. She could skin a raccoon
in minutes. Revealing the flesh (actually a purpling pink) easy
as snapping a guinea neck. She would have given anything
to wake up in a new skin, though hers was delightful in the light.
But what did I know?
I'm not the first to ask that question. The toil took its toll
and though her face barely wrinkled, her knees and elbows
    darkened
into the skin I wear now. Roughened into the heels I scratch
against my husband's calves in bed, because I don't listen.
I refuse to wear shoes. I'm as country as she didn't want me to be.
I loved the way she smelled. Like outdoors. Like new sheets. Hot
grease and rifle burn. Raisin pie with coffee. Front porch. Corn cob.
Her skin held all she did her best to scrub free. Scrubbed so hard
it liked to take the skin right off her.
Which was what she wanted. To have it off on her own terms,
not the eyes, all the eyes that demonized her: *Unsightly. Dirty.*
Unseemly. She saved for lace, for crinolines, for pretty gloves and
wide-brimmed hats to hide her skin. Mine is mottled. Stress-
    blemished,
but soft as hers and I know it. Easy enough to remove. As a girl I
    tried
to burn it off. To find the pink I was convinced lay beneath.
I'm not the first. I wore scarves she made to cover the evidence
of my curiosity. I give myself over

to the lotions of the day. Disparage the oils she did not love
but felt she needed. She'd stroke my cheek and say, "good baby"
and I'd feel good in my skin, in that moment.
I'd hold her tight some nights and whisper, "You are the prettiest,"
and she'd feel good, in hers. I want to forget, but I have my mirrors.
And there she is, shadowed, in a sun-struck field.

VIEVEE FRANCIS

Souvenirs

for my father

Through the mirror
I can see you reading
your new testament before bed,
putting it away in the dresser drawer
where you keep

the tin box of foreign coins
and the hand-tinted postcards
of Italy
you brought home from the Navy
in 1954.

We lie awake
my brother and I
listening to you on the back steps
singing
only half to yourself
a snatch of an old miner's song
that goes:

up every day
in the dawn's early light

to go down in a hole
where it's already night

it's already night
boys it's already night

and through the window
I watch the fireflies
among the trees,
which,

you told us once,
were dead people lighting cigarettes.

TONY CRUNK

Street View: Google Earth: Lakeview Avenue

There it is, or isn't, my grandfather's garage
torn down some time in the last few years.
What's left is a car-park of small pebbles

and now, just off the phone with a cousin, my uncle
has died, leaving me with his memories,
the silliness of his humor I take with me

for everyone I meet, because in this world
there's already enough pain. I don't need
to bring it with me to every dinner party.

When I was a kid, being funny meant something
special, yet, left me feeling irreverent,
with a sense of loss, as if I had done so much wrong

because I was not serious about anything
except what made you laugh.
Or entertained you, at all expense.

In this hand-built garage that used to be,
there was a serious nature to all things: the vise
that held everything so tight, the boat

on a trailer, dusty from the winter
hibernation, fishing poles erect
as Prussian lances, lures quiet and taut

at the end of a steel leader, the long wooden
row of workbenches for hammering
out what was broken, and not funny at all.

WILLIAM WALSH

Sunder

A last rock-skip hurlstorm (crazing river-glass)
the closest they ever were.

•

In right lockstitch
snared and split some fire-supper cooked on sticks.

•

By dawn the older brother took to chucking
what bottle-frags he could find and crud-oysters across.
The (high-pitched) younger blacked our waters

with a yowl.

•

Lord the sound such as rose from him
carried so—
Carved
into us. Clings.

•

Hadn't they clung tooth and claw to branch and bark.
—Came a man (and truck) to take them off.

•

Dieseled those boys off
away
some say somewheres upcountry,
inland.

Where it was they landed (why) nobody not them knows.

No body not them knows
just how they humped and grubbled home
what road they'd graved what woods criss-crossed
which creeks which trains they'd hopped who helped.

Came safe home sure   *but blank as houses.*
Came safe home   —as him.   —and him.

—as (evermore) not them.

ATSURO RILEY

Target

Dear Arrowhead water, dear feather boa, dear father
and mother with the toddler and cart full of candles:

I wanted to tell you the sky swished open its doors
this morning, the whole shebang slid by on felt,

and I entered the mythic fires of stoicism,
bore my nakedness in the manner of Shackleton,

defiantly ignorant. For I know that Target, centerless
like new pedagogies, loves the good good,

loves punishment somehow instructing
a niche audience. That's me. I love to finger

the Milano-style whatnot, bend the necks
of five-headed floor lamps. Yes, I love you dearly,

dear church of the cherished storage bin,
dear Cheerios and the bowl to drown you in,

dear warehouse sky, dear reindeer aiming the beads
of your eyes at my impulse buys. Once, I shot a gun

in the desert, laid it down in the sand, and said
a small prayer to prayers of small sizes.

Years later, we navigated the marked-downs,
the Doritos safe in Mylar pillows,

thought we'd stripped ourselves clean
of desire's burrs and foxtails, even as popcorn

promised low-sodium transubstantiation.
But we were *registering*, the word itself green, bearded,

so aimed our fantastic machines at the crock
pot and bath rug, at the iPod snug in its skin.

We dressed ourselves in the warmth of that small space
heater, fed the nuisance of class consciousness

little biscuits. How cloudless, how terrible and lucid
the distances we traveled for our dear wedding guests—

dear, which my Italian friend uses in that foreign way,
as in, *That pair of pants is too dear*. And how dear, how sheer

the night, we thought, dearly beloved, outside the Target,
the headlights of all those cars trained on us.

CHAD DAVIDSON

The Tavern Trees

—Fairfield, Tennessee

Having forced the stiff U.S. Mail flag up
and left the card crackling among cricket nymphs,
the wheel ruts' little rocks nibbling at my soles,
the cattle grate a memory, a lock installed
to forbid locals from riding donuts on the lawn
or chucking empties in the boondocks,
from which fireflies still drowse into the grasp
like spirits, Eliza says, like will-o'-the-wisp—
all at once they sweep up from the grass:
hackberry, coffee, sweet gum, ash, and beech,
centuries of speechlessness pitched to a high,
unfiltered exactitude my praise stabs at
even as they fall back to papery, aromatic stars
and elephant ears fruited savagely as maces.

DANIELLE CHAPMAN

Telephoning

Dirt-stopped, eary mussel shells were strewn
across alluvium jigsawed by the sun.
Barefoot, I waited, saw Jack Langston dunk
all comers in the Cache. God's champion.
Tall cypress knees loomed gray along the bank
like tombstones. As the line shrank,

words from "Jesus on the Mainline" rang
inside my head. (Sister Lila had sung
a couple rounds to start the ceremony.)
Call him up, rolling off a Southern tongue,
sounded like "call them up," reminding me
of Uncle Paul, of all I couldn't be

now that I was Langston's kind of Christian.
Tangly red hair like dodder in the sun,
Paul taught me how to call them up: He stole
his mama's antique hand-crank telephone—
a little generator, powerful
enough to be our magic fishing reel.

With rubber seats and boots, we'd float the Cache,
cathedral-quiet if not for chirp or splash.
Mirrored dimly in the river's brown,
tupelos towered—cypress, gum, and ash.
We'd hook two twelve-gauge wires up to the phone
and drop them in the water twelve feet down.

Finally, when I was twelve, my uncle said,
"Here, man this winder—you ain't no little kid."
The fish lived through the shock but couldn't swim
for minutes, only float. I cranked like mad.
As Paul took hold of the dip net, here they came:
flathead, blue cat, buffalo, and bream . . .

It was time. My feet went clean invisible
and read the riverbed's treacherous Braille.
Langston covered my nose and mouth with white,
then braced my back and said, "Surrender all."
In a wet rush, I felt my blood ignite
and shivered as I rose electrified.

GREG BROWNDERVILLE

Testament

Our agreement cuts us out of each other's wills.
Nonetheless, I bequeath to you
a Rube Goldberg Self-Operating Napkin
because of how much simpler honesty would have been—
you, consumed by the future wiping of your own chin.
You lit explosives. You manipulated both weight
and gravity. You used death's scythe to cut the string.
I leave you a Jesus Bug, balanced
like a hand on a stagnancy of rainwater.
I know you hate spiders. This isn't one.
I leave you the world aiming its moonlight
on the black, nervous ocean of fish
who have nowhere else to go.
All civilities to you. A summer sky grown yellow at the edges.
Make good use of this page of onion skin.

JULIE FUNDERBURK

The Theft

A few weeks into first semester
at the central Pennsylvania college
I partied myself out of
in less than a year, I stole
my roommate's girlfriend with a kiss
one starless night outside our dorm—
or put more truly, she threw a leg across
and borrowed me, like an unchained
bike, to ride away from him.
Even though she dropped me, too,
not long after—or let's say
she leaned me gently against
a tree—it nags me to this day
that he packed for the family farm,
never returned. Thirty years and still
I picture him behind the wheel
(sky the color of denim, horses
in the distance, grazing on the distance),
cursing me every mile from school
to home. Her name was Judy, his, Eric,
I can't remember mine. I can call up
little more than ramen soups, stacked
higher than books on our shelves, the guitar
I picked at all the time, a musical scab,
and his scuffed-up golf clubs in the corner
(he'd made the team with ease).
He scrawled ASSHOLE in Magic Marker
on my book bag before he left,
and of course I couldn't blame him
but blamed him all the same,
telling the guys on the floor
what a rube he was, a yokel,
until he entered our collective memory,
then our communal forgetting. Judy,
I have no doubt, runs a law firm now,

her dark eyes trained on justice,
and some nights, awake in bed,
I think of Eric as a tall, thick-wristed kid
just out of high school, who could drive
a tractor, track a deer, and knock
a golf ball farther than any man
for a hundred miles. In my dream for him,
he keeps his feelings locked inside
a cabin in the woods, but lets them out
at last—stunned and blinking—
when he meets the perfect woman
(what would you say?) working
the ticket booth at a summer fair.
But other times, when dreams won't do,
I fear he married the girl he took
to prom. They get on fine, steadily
if blandly, raise some kids, until the day
the vision returns, and Eric sees himself
at the second-story window, peering
down at Judy and me, leaning close.
That's when, in disgust, he grits
his teeth and throws a hand
in the air, dismissing the life he chose
with the gesture of a golfer
tossing up a pinch of grass
to test the inclination of the wind.

GREG FRASER

A Theory of Everything

It has something to do with invisible string
rippling out across a universal sunset,
wrapping us up like the perfect brown corded package.

Something to do with the vibration of stars—
how they flicker in tune with each other, humming cosmically.
And though I've never seen this reported anywhere

I also believe it has something to do with dogs.
For who else has such capacity to forgive
an entirely other species? Well, yes, God

but I don't mess around with God.
So in my theory, the wet nose of a dog
fits in the space where our heart has been cut out.

And after dogs, the pure yellow of lemons,
the affection small children hold for Band-aids, the urge
to touch a stranger's bald head.

It all has a place in the Theory.
Name it and I will hang it on the clothesline.
Name it, I will chop it up for soup.

What's not to believe, anyway, in a theory
that has room enough for all other theories,
even those that say this Theory is shit?

Sure, the vibration of strings we cannot measure.
And yes, the strings are so fine we haven't seen them yet.
One might surmise that this is not about strings, but our desire for
    strings.

You too are welcome at this Party of Everything.
Come to my house, into my house. We will speak

of aqueducts and whiskers, we will eat

brown bread and touch our feet under the table.
You can tell me we are not connected,
that there is nothing out there holding us together.

I will tug your ear and peck you softly on the lips.

MARY CROCKETT HILL

Three Vultures on the Blacktop to Memphis

Why are all the roads in this part of Alabama
        named after men? There's Woody Skelton Road,
Lester Patterson and Murk Montgomery Roads,
        and what the hell is "Murk" short for? Murky? Mercury?
These are roads that time has passed, their sides luxuriant

        with kudzu, Queen Anne's lace, pink mallow, and golden
fields of yarrow. We drive past abandoned gas stations
        and their sad cafes, vines crawling over the windows
where men and women drank cups of coffee and ate plates
        of eggs sunny side up with white toast, grits, and bacon

before taking off north to Tupelo or south to Tuscaloosa,
        and one thing the South has plenty of is roadside varmints—
raccoons, possums, armadillos, not to mention feral cats
        and stray dogs—so every so often we pass one of them
with his guts open on the side of the road, a neon *memento mori*

        for those who would care to take their thoughts
in that direction, and on a straightaway you can see
        a confraternity of vultures pecking away at a carcass,
like the monks I saw once in Florence who came to pick up
        a tourist who had fainted in front of the Duomo

without, of course, the bloody possum entrails in their mouths,
        and the vultures don't fly away until the last moment,
and we whiz on by, but I can't help but think about their place
        in the order of things, how they carry away the dead body
and use it for their needs, and when I see their nests high in a pine
        tree,

        they seem like little gods of disintegration as we all are
in our own three-alarm fires of napalm and bitter address,

        such as I feel every time I look at my next door neighbor
who sawed off twenty feet of the beautiful arching limb
        of the two-hundred-year-old oak tree in our back yard

because it was brushing against his fence that might last twenty
        years if he's lucky, and every time I see the amputated limb
or the five pickup trucks in his front yard, a fury rises up
        inside me, and I'm trying to practice *ksanti*, or forbearance,
one of the six perfections in Buddhism, but not having much luck,

        and how does it all add up? The tree, my neighbor,
his fence, and who am I in that equation—the vulture
        or the possum or maybe I am just the road or even the
    raccoon,
who made it to the other side and is digging in the dumpster
        behind the Burger King in Fayette, Alabama, not thinking

about much, but with a sense of smell like nobody's business,
        and it's the stink of the world that drives me crazy,
not just the jasmine, but the rotting flesh of trees and animals,
        the reminders to take it all in because I'm heading
somewhere on this misbegotten stretch of road and going fast.

BARBARA HAMBY

Toshno

Marina is trying to describe Raskolnikov's interior state
        and uses the word *toshno*, which she says comes
from the same word as "to vomit," which makes me think
        of Sartre's *La Nausée* and the German *Weltschmertz*,
but Sasha says, it also has an element of nostalgia or longing,
        thinking about how at one time you felt happy
but can no longer feel that way, though from my perch
        it's difficult not to see Raskolnikov's malady
as a combination of poor nutrition and too much philosophy,
        or at least that's how I think of myself in my twenties,
thin from vegetarianism and grinding anxiety, maddened
        by my parents' fundamentalism, shucked off
but lurking in the corners of my brain, though in the ensuing days
        I begin to think of other emotions that English has
no word to express: to take something bad, such as
        a firing, broken heart, insult, and turn it
into something so luminous that you are grateful
        to the ex-wife, nasty co-worker, unfaithful lover
for the sneer, slag, the stab in the back. Or the feeling
        of sadness after finishing a book you adore
because the thrill of first reading those glorious words
        is gone forever. Or when you realize someone
hates you, so a person, who was once nothing to you,
        is now the focus of your attention. Walking
down the avenues of St. Petersburg or lying in an Italian bed,
        you think about the river you have just seen
or the painting that until now has been a two-inch square in a book,
        but that afternoon you saw the wall covered
with a luminous fresco, colors so vivid that the crazy
        painter could have walked in from the next room
covered with red and green and you wouldn't have been surprised,
        but soon you will be sitting in your garden at home,
watching the wrens make a nest in a paint can hooked to a tree,
        and then in thirty or so years, if you're lucky,
you will be so old your body will be giving up, shoulders bent,

with no taste for food, and what is the word for that,
and will you know it when it's whispered in your ear?

BARBARA HAMBY

The Tradition

Aster. Nasturtium. Delphinium. We thought
Fingers in dirt meant it was our dirt, learning
Names in heat, in elements classical
Philosophers said could change us. *Stargazer.*
Foxglove. Summer seemed to bloom against the will
Of the sun, which news reports claimed flamed hotter
On this planet than when our dead fathers
Wiped sweat from their necks. *Cosmos. Baby's Breath.*
Men like me and my brothers filmed what we
Planted for proof we existed before
Too late, sped the video to see blossoms
Brought in seconds, color you expect in poems
Where the world ends, everything cut down.
John Crawford. Eric Garner. Mike Brown.

JERICHO BROWN

The Transfiguration of a Certain Plowman

By afternoon, the sun had gone
from the hollow, so I walked up
to the head and there in the open field
the last of the daylight found me.
There's a hickory stump up there
and a turned-up mule shoe,
like a lazy man, leans back
against it. Even before the shoe
fell off, the man behind the mule
had faced a four-fold truth—
U, U, U, U—
when he held the plow and the hooves came up,
and the whole communion of man and mule
and plow tilted and sung in the furrows.
The man had broken ground, and then
there wasn't any more to break.
But broken ground will never not
be ground; it is turned and then returns
in its time: it changes to continue.
Truth is, the man who ran the plow
is dead, and so are his descendants,
and I will die some day, but that pate
of hilltop up the hollow ringed
by a crown of cedars will not be done.
So I go to the broken garden to be
accused and broken down and changed—
that day I lay down in the grass
and dreamed. The bugs crawled over me,
and a roan-colored moth lit
on my out-stretched hand and winked
like an eye and blinked, staring at all
I was and wasn't. Beyond the moth
the stump and the iron U waited,

like a throat holding onto a word,
a stiff word unsaid though known
forever, even across the wastes
of time uncounted the word is known.
I said I dreamed that day and I did;
the last fine day of the last
season, something was ending, not me,
not yet, but maybe something in me,
and I wondered what remains and what
is over. I don't know. So I dreamed
for a tiny timeless moment, long
enough to see the man before
with his ax and his mule, and how the shoe
fell off dragging the felled tree
down the hill to be squared and pegged
and turned into a timber to build
the house I live in now, without a mule
to my name, though that may change as my heart
is changing, letting out its ache
without reason, not in hope
of anything. It's happening.
And so the mule shoe was a symbol,
but the mule was a mule, and the tree was felled,
and I had heard the nameless voice
emanating, naming it all
informally, in second person.

MAURICE MANNING

Trying Not to Cry Before Dinner

The backyard is frozen
in patches of mud and silver grass,
a garden of broken TVs and rotting lumber.
You promised to build a tool shed
but the planks have sunk into the mud.
The kitchen is filling with steam.
Corn silk clogs the disposal, the stems
of mushrooms and broccoli float in the sink.
I count TVs through the window
as a thin fog rises from the piles
of parts of things that are no longer useful.
The fog climbs the clapboards,
tendrils creep up the window, a ghost of ivy.
You test the air like tasting soup,
using a low word like a spoon.
You clear your throat,
say you have felt me turn cold
like a voice after a long pause on the telephone.
You turn the corn with a fork
as the water boils.
You say to the corn, "Don't cry, don't cry."
A sudden, invisible rain begins pushing the fog back,
pushing the fog down off the window,
flooding the tires and the ditches you dug
for tulip bulbs and golf.
I tell you I am going to sit on the porch.
I hold very still in the porch swing and wait
for you to come outside and light a cigarette,
small comfort against the rain
and the temperature dropping
like a hand after a wave.

JOSEPHINE YU

Valentine

I hope your father built a treehouse in the soft
shade below the creek. I hope it glimmered there, between two
poplars. I hope you stood at your mother's sleeve
while she fixed madeleines for breakfast. It was Easter.
All six of your aunts adored you. For your country project
you picked Tunisia because of its peanut shape. Which was your
    first rock show?
Mine was Milli Vanilli. I hope you licked the ends of your colored
pencils. Also, that you carried a Trapper Keeper. The first time a girl
touched you, I hope you had graham crumbs on your mouth. I hope
she wore her brother's hunting coat, latchless.

Do you also dislike beets? I hope so. I hope you're
reading all the classics, like *Moby-Dick*. When the preacher
climbs the ladder made of ropes? That's the best. I did that
once, at an amusement park. I believe the stars get brighter
when it's cold. Do you like riding in convertibles? I like
riding in convertibles. I like how sunflowers turn themselves
into big radios. I used to live where canola oil's from. I used
to eat fried zucchini flowers and tomato salad. What do you
like for breakfast? Do you listen to BBC News? When you make
someone a sandwich, I hope you trim the casings from each
slice of salami. No one likes to eat those.

I try to think of what you'll need from Walgreens.
Maybe you've got contacts. In which case, you can just use
my solution. What diseases run in your family? Will we have to worry
about strokes? I'll probably live to be quite old. I hope you'll let me
lay out your pajamas. Not every day, but sometimes. Will you eat
    bran patties
for breakfast then? What about those S-cookies? Those come
    from Sicily.
I've seen them in the shops. I've seen women in gold slingbacks
on the bus. That's OK, but I hope we'll have our own car. I know
    a church

with a dark ceiling. The Normans built it. It's sad until you drop coins into this special lamp: clink, clink. After that, it's different, see.

KIKI PETROSINO

Visiting a Lost Aunt at the Jefferson Davis Hotel, Elkton

All my father said when he hung up the phone was, "Well I guess Wanda has found her way back." We wait for him now in the small lobby while he looks for somebody to help us. There's a coat tree, a newspaper rack, a cigarette machine. There's a big chair in the corner where they shine shoes, but nobody's shining shoes on Sunday. I have never been inside a hotel before.

He comes back, leads us up the carpeted stairs and into a hallway — a window open at the end of it, a thin veil of rainwater rolling down off the eaves. We find number 28 and knock.

I have never seen Aunt Wanda before. She opens the door, wearing shorts on Sunday morning, and we go in. She hugs my mother, then my father – she's sorry we had to come all that way in the rain — sets a suitcase in the closet to get it out of the way —she would've called last night but was out late with some people she had looked up.

There are only two chairs, so my mother sits on the bed with my brother and me. Aunt Wanda is sorry it's so hot in there, but they didn't even have a window fan they could give her. She would offer us something to drink, but there isn't any ice. They all light cigarettes, sharing the one ashtray. Rainwater is rolling off the eaves outside her window, too.

Aunt Wanda talks a while about my brother and me, reaches over and pats my ankle, my mother smoothes my hair back off my forehead. My father tells about his new job, driving mail to Bowling Green. Aunt Wanda tells about somebody in Louisville — I guess he would have been my uncle. She asks my father about their cousin Dewey. She asks about the home place, but doesn't think she'll have time to go out.

Finally, my father tells her how their father, my grandfather, died. At the VA Hospital in Nashville, in a room overlooking the parking lot. Calling out for three days that his legs were on fire. Calling out for water.

Aunt Wanda shakes the ashtray, watching the ashes and butts sift back and forth. I'm watching, too, wishing I were home. I would spend the afternoon picking the shells of katydids off of trees. Dropping them one by one into the gutter stream that would be running by the sidewalk. Walking along beside them as they floated down the street — my ghost fleet, vanishing through the grating of the storm drain on the corner.

TONY CRUNK

The Wake

James Abbott McNeill Whistler in Venice

I.

Huddled in the gondola, tired of numb fumbling
with plate and stylus, he abandons the eleventh etching
for dovebelly brown paper and the swipe of chalk.

The laundrettes have come down to the doorway,
dipping their wicker baskets into the water.
A balcony above divulges their linens.

His betrothed Rialto, all state and arch, is waiting.
But his line wants to stay here and seduce this alley,
occupy each molded shadow of stairstep. Shiver thin

then thick. Caress the bend of waists slendered by work.
The girls fold sheets corner to corner. They stretch
and blend. When the color comes it is arterial,

cut wrist let loose upon the world—
brick ochred mandarin, windowpanes frocked
olive green, a sky fleshed with morning—

until a crowd of starlings descends on the balustrade.
He picks up the black charcoal, starts to adulterate
pink horizon with their chattering forms. Stops.

The girls, they are finishing now, they are yawning,
and the gondolier mutters for his lunch.
As they pull away from the canal's slick edge

the water holds, for a breath, the shape of their passing.
He knows no plate could manage that wet cleave,
no pastel give more than the dimmest echo

of that blue lack. Thank god it is only a moment
before the sea is again seamless, complete. Something
he can honor. Something he can own.

II.

At first her cough was a poor thread—slender, inconsistent—
something to worry about over the dinner roast, something
to pull loose with Darjeeling tea and honey. She poured

and pulled and out it came, and out, and out, into full ropes
that draped her. An obscene rosary of hacking. Then they knew
a deeper thing, something bone-bred, had unraveled.

Nights like this he comes home and she is already asleep,
cushioned in gold velvet long since worn away at the arms,
limp stitchwork dangling from one palm. He is inkstained,

freezing, and still the silk jutting from his pocket matches
the band on his hat. A man of precision. He wishes
he could warm her, a blanket of muscle striated with gin,

but she can no longer manage the stairs to the bedroom.
Another night, the Duveneck boys will get a card game going.
Another night he'll call Maud, who oils her breasts in lavender,

who knows the price at which each plate sells. But tonight
he pulls his own chair to his wife and takes out the sketchpad.
He sets aside blue and white, sharpens yellow and grey.

Just as he drew the palazzo from its crumbling dock,
beadstringers from their murky alley, so he lifts her body
beyond a room of dirty porcelain and leather.

He traces the scape of her, calves lithe and unspent.
She does not stir as he crosses her ankles. He is humming, intent,
but she does not stir. A spider's line for her hair—skittering,

loose, black charcoal spinning itself away. He is
her own best hangman. He will call it by her name.
He will not fill in the cocoon of her face.

SANDRA BEASLEY

Wal*Mart Supercenter

God Bless America says the bumper sticker on the racer-red
Rascal scooter that accidentally cuts me off in the Walmart
    parking lot
after a guy in a tricked-out jeep with rims like chrome pinwheels tries
to pick me up by honking, all before I make it past the automatic
    doors
waiting to accept my unwashed hair, my flip-flops, my lounge pants.

The old man on the scooter waves, sports a straw boater banded
    in blue & white,
and may or may not be the official greeter, but everyone here sure
    is friendly—
even the faces of plastic bags, which wink yellow and crinkle with
    kindness,
sound like applause when they brush the legs of shoppers carrying
    them
to their cars. In Port Charlotte, a woman's body was found in a Jetta

in a Walmart parking lot. In a Walmart parking lot in Springfield,
a macaque monkey named Charlie attacked an eight-year-old girl.
I am a Walmart shopper, a tract-house dweller—the developments
you can see clearly from every highway in America that's not
    jammed up
on farmland or pinned in by mountains. I park my car at a slant
    in the lot,

hugged tight by my neighbors' pickups. I drive my enormous cart
through the aisles and fill it with Pampers, tube socks, juice boxes,
    fruit.
In the parking lot of the McAllen Walmart, a woman tried to sell six
Bengal tiger cubs to a group of Mexican day laborers. A man
    carjacked
a woman in the parking lot of the West Mifflin Walmart, then ran

under a bridge and disappeared. Which is to say that the world

we expect to see looks hewn from wood, is maybe two lanes wide,
has readily identifiable produce, and the one we've got has
     jackknifed itself
on the side of the interstate and keeps skidding. The one we've
     got has clouds
traveling so fast across the sky it's like they're tied to an electric
     current.

But electricity is the same for everybody. It comes in the top of
     your head
and goes out your shoes, which will walk through these automatic
     doors.
In the Corbin Walmart parking lot a woman with a small amount
     of cash
was arrested for getting in and out of trucks. A man stepped out
     of his car
in the Columbus Walmart parking lot, and shot himself. I get in
     the checkout line

behind a lighted number on a pole. The man in front of me
     jangles coins
in his pocket, rocks back and forth on his heels. The girl in front
     of him
carefully peels four moist dimes from her palm to pay for a small
     container
of honey-mustard dipping sauce. In the parking lot of the
     LaFayette Walmart,
grandparents left their disabled two-year-old grandson sitting in a
     shopping cart

and drove away. Employees in the parking lot at the La Grange
     Walmart
found a box containing seven abandoned kittens. I am not a
     Christian or
prone to idioms, but when the cashier says she is grateful for small
     mercies,
I nod in assent. *Kyrie eleison, Christe eleison.* The Latin root of
     mercy

means price paid, wages, merchandise, though now we use it as

compassion shown to a person in a position of powerlessness,
and sometimes forgiveness towards a person with no right
to claim it. God is merciful and gracious, but not just.
In the Walmart parking lot in Stockton, a man considered armed
and dangerous attacked his wife, beating her unconscious.

A couple tried to sell their six-month-old for twenty-five bucks
to buy meth in the Salinas Walmart parking lot. We who are in
    danger,
remember: mercy has a human heart. Mercy with her tender
    mitigations,
slow to anger and great in loving-kindness, with her blue
    employee's smock
emblazoned with *How may I help you?* Someone in this place have
    mercy on us.

ERIKA MEITNER

Wandered, The

—*Glover Park, Washington, DC*

Tucked under the pre-dawn silence,
there is a boy laid like garnish on the raw
sidewalk—*some measure of dead* I assume.
I learn to walk as my neighbors would: stepping
a sharp arc out and around his splayed legs.

Even in winter's steady palm,
he seems not to pulse. The stone beneath
his head bears nothing but his head—
maybe sleep, but no sign
that I should risk his waking.
I alert no one—let the breathless lay
at 3 a.m. Enter your house, lock your door,
and maybe thumb your memory for prayers.

> Likely, the call comes in
> from the mother in the house
> behind the tree
> beneath which this unknown sleeps.

Police lights' familiar searing drags me
through my window curtains—anxious to witness
how such things unfold in Georgetown.
A voice, distorted by the cruiser p.a., calls
"Sir, please move." *Fools, he is no more.*
"Sir, you need to move." There is no third
warning. I fear they will come
knocking for information, alibis. I'll say
ask the stone—the only thing on the block
that dares listen to him, consider his weight.
Instead, they slide out the cruiser,
rouse him with a shake, and lead him
slowly inside the patrol car
like coroners of dreams.

KYLE DARGAN

Watch

Time, carnal cradle,
do we sleep in the feminine?

If so, why instead this casket
of sexless moonlight,

second hands gathering drams
of unspoken words,

the window's ladder of shadow?
Interior of the letter "O,"

tick of a starving dialect,
latch the bomb makes, nursing oblivion:

I am out-waiting them.
Pen scratch, carcass stalking

the diphthong hours of near-dawn,
is this suffering? I know

these instants until you arrive
as my rivals. Defeat them with your coming.

LISA RUSS SPAAR

The Water

In the morning the water waits like a deckhand,
a persistent curl against the shore,

who won't back down, take no, or be denied.
It is there under the wharf and soon under

the house, whoring with any swamp rat
or snake. It rings cypress knees with pearls—

it dreams under the sun like cut cane,
throwing back the salt you wash away,

then wearing pilings down to air.
Your houses wade on stilts tall as pillars,

their sheet-metal skulls bared to a mildewed
sky. Against the fallen trees rain and lapping

tide meet, slapping of nets and fish and
naked children pulling driftwood boats

in one joyful noise around your sleep.
In the afternoon the water is there, only more,

browner and grayer, no sweeping seaweed or foam,
just its presence farther up your shore,

like a dull brother-in-law in front of TV.
He means something to somebody—

but not you, not just now. Its slow wake seems
harmless, the litany of waves before a storm

rolling benignly ashore. Intoxicating!
And then it is there, all gray length of it,

rich sex of it, it wants you so badly,
it pounds at the door, Let me take

your smallness, your jetties, your broad
coasts, your loam. It gathers

at night beyond the curtain of mosquitoes,
darker than the shut-down sky,

the boarded-up clouds. Its desire
thrums like an idling outboard. Ignore

it, and it tows itself into your dreams. It's
everywhere, every chance, all the time.

It is more certain than death or love.
It must have been conceived by death and love.

When the last silt sinks under your feet,
you will have to walk out on this water.

MARTHA SERPAS

The Way Back

I know an axe and a turtle's shell.
I know the day I won

A silver watch in school
Then came home with my father

To tell my mother her mother had died.
I know the way

My mother slapped him
And let her nails

Linger. Bleeding,
He smiled to teach me:

We slap whom we love.
I know a boy and a turtle

Each time he held it, it withdrew.
And my aunt was a sea

And two borders removed.
I know the summer she spent waiting

For a visa, sitting in bed, knees
Bent to hold a book she was reading.

No one had told her
Her mother had died.

When she arrived
She smiled and kissed me.

I said nothing. She wailed and
My uncle slapped her once.

I know the sisters wanted
And the boy also wanted.

To see the body
Inside its shell.

There were shovels by the grave.
There was an axe in the garden.

FADY JOUDAH

What I Want Is Simple

La terre est bleue comme une orange.

—Paul Éluard

Begin with the fuchsia dress
I wore the night the scent
of storm threaded the brief
wind gusting away its hem
from my thighs—begin
with this orange, moldy
in its yellow bowl by the window.
Days it has rested there,
glossy as a child after a summer
spent outside. Days I have
looked past it—to crumbling
brick walls of other buildings,
smoke from a chimney, engraved
for a moment on gray sky.
It bewilders me to have looked
at this piece of fruit without
seeing it grow its own blue
shroud. Now you, too, are
gone. In that photo, I am
a waist towards which black
hair spills. You smile towards
someone or something I can't
see. I want back that night you
pulled me into your lap, insisted
I stay there. I want the elegant
hinge of your wrist, the way you
were always both body & bird.
The way you were never & always
listening. You were wearing
a green sweater. There is
so little to take back, receive,
give. There is, somewhere, your
green sweater. What I want is

simple: you, alive, like the day
we bought an orange like the one
I lift now from its bowl to throw
out. How many times I have looked
at the world and turned away.

TARFIA FAIZULLAH

When at a Certain Party in NYC

Wherever you're from sucks,
and wherever you grew up sucks,
and everyone here lives in a converted
chocolate factory or deconsecrated church
without an ugly lamp or souvenir coffee cup
in sight, but only carefully edited objects like
the Lacanian soap dispenser in the kitchen
that looks like an industrial age dildo, and
when you rifle through the bathroom
looking for a spare tampon, you discover
that even their toothpaste is somehow more
desirable than yours. And later you go
with a world famous critic to eat a plate
of sushi prepared by a world famous chef from
Sweden and the roll is conceived to look like
"a strand of pearls around a white throat," and is
so confusingly beautiful that it makes itself
impossible to eat. And your friend back home—
who says the pioneers who first settled
the great asphalt parking lot of our
middle, were not in fact heroic, but really
the chubby ones who lacked the imagination
to go all the way to California—it could be that
she's on to something. Because, admit it,
when you look at the people on these streets,
the razor-blade women with their strategic bones
and the men wearing Amish pants with
interesting zippers, it's pretty clear that you
will never cut it anywhere that constitutes
a where, that even ordering a pint of tuna salad in
a deli is an illustrative exercise in self-doubt.
So when you see the dogs on the high-rise elevators
practically tweaking, panting all the way down
from the 19th floor to the 1st, dying to get on
with their long planned business of snuffling

trash or peeing on something to which all day
they've been looking forward, what you want is
to be on the fastest Conestoga home, where the other
losers live and where the tasteless azaleas are,
as we speak, half-heartedly exploding.

ERIN BELIEU

White Castle

I don't remember if the man
was white or if she was.
I was aware at a young six of the strange
sight they made by sitting across from one another
for dinner in a fast food joint surrounded by white.
I'd never seen a mixed couple, and thought
it wasn't possible, not because of whatever small town
sense made it taboo, but because I believed
it was like having a door both opened
and closed at the same time. As far as I know,
nothing happened in the dining room
but eating and staring. I don't remember what my parents
said or did. I'd like to think they told me to stop staring,
or that they didn't feel like the rest
of the restaurant who ate square burgers and greasy fries
from white paper cartons and stared at the couple
while they ate from the same, stared at one another.
We watched like they performed
magic tricks with love. It must have been a few months
before my teenager cousin, while he hid
behind a tree, made us—his younger sister and me—
yell at a black boy who walked by our grandmother's house.
I didn't know the word, but knew
the feeling of it. I was ashamed
right after that word came out of my mouth,
and when the boy, about my age, turned to stare at us,
two white girls higher up than the street he was walking,
he just looked. I never told anyone
about what I thought when I saw the couple.
I'd like to say that what I saw when he opened the door
for her was a couple leaving a restaurant.
And I never told anyone what I said, never spoke
of it again. I am bound to that act, that boy,

who I don't remember in any specifics,
in a way that I cannot say.

KATIE CHAPLE

XLVIII from *Bucolics*

when I chop wood you warm me twice
you send a wind then send the cool
behind it Boss we work together
side by side when I drop the share
in the dirt you make it sing you give
a song to turning dirt we keep
some big irons in the fire don't we
Boss we keep it stoked there's wood
in the wood box there's a kettle on
the stove there's a whisper coming from
the kettle whenever something's doing
there's always something else that's just
the way it is side by side Boss
just like I said O one plus one
is too as in also Boss always
also O one thing also then
another that's the way you are
the way you always are I think
your favorite number Boss is two

MAURICE MANNING

Yestermorrow

Hallelujah, it's nobody's birthday!
Nobody's wedding and nobody's wake!
For once the glib calendar's dumb.
These brave hours have sloughed off their date.

No unions are striking, no voters are polled,
though if anything dawn has come early.
While the coffee is yet to be ground,
our displeasures dissolve prematurely.

We're a people with bleachers to get to,
outlets to enter, entrees to eat,
yet this morning it's clear to anyone:
nothing's planned and there's nowhere to be.

If the wind at the back of our minds is persuasive,
routine destinations feel wrong.
We wander outside in pajamas
to stand at the edge of our lawns.

Hallelujah that here on mortality's turf
the daily's been soundly defeated!
The diaries are shredded inside us.
Invincible dockets retreated.

Any vows we have made to each other
melt away in our mouths like confections
and at once they're replaced by the knowledge
that at last we're immune to deception.

The day picks up its skirts with its eyes closed,
eventful, though nothing will count.
I hear fireworks rebound one street over.
The de Whitts, in their front yard, make out.

As local balloonists are coasting their baskets
to rest in the neighborhood park
our children eject from the tire swings
and slowly tear heaven apart.

Even when dusk sizzles through the azaleas
the day feels unwilling to end.
Stars flicker back out in the cypress.
The moon seems inclined to descend.

Hallelujah the TVs refuse to report
any scandals, invasions, or earthquakes!
What's next we'll discover in time
when eternity turns into Thursday.

GEORGE DAVID CLARK

Appendix:
What is The South? What is
Southern poetry?

The South is a contradiction. It is mountains and swamps, histories and futures, beauty and hatred, someplace and every place. At times I feel the South is an inextricable part of who I am and determines much of how I see the rest of the world. And then there are moments when I do not—cannot—understand the place I grew up. But the South is my home. It isn't always easy, as love is not always easy. Perhaps more than a contradiction, then, the South represents reconciliation—finding peace in accepting one's flaws. When I close my eyes, I see the South as I see moments just before dawn, when darkness still lingers in the air, the promise of light flits just below the horizon, and above all else there is the certainty of another day.

—CHAD ABUSHANAB

Many people who talk about "The South" in the context of literature refer to landscape. I was born and raised in South Carolina, and in my experience the Southern landscape is the suburban dinner table, and its primary features are silence and denial. Silence as thick as morning swamp fog. Denial as heavy as centuries-old chains. I try to convert silence into poetry. I try to confront denial so ensconced and monolithic that it still enslaves. Sometimes I think I succeed a little; other times I think the cicadas do a better job.

—DAN ALBERGOTTI

I grew up in Virginia. I've spent a significant portion of my 30s visiting Mississippi. Each warily eyes the other's particular Southern legacy. People argue whether Texas and Florida, my next most-loved states, "count." There is no monolithic South; there never was. So why do I feel it in my bones when among Southerners?

Why does my voice and posture change? Why am I a funnier, more relaxed version of myself? Why does a roadside stand of boiled peanuts give me such joy? Why is all my best dancing to the hill country blues? I use the codification of "Southern" not in an attempt to understand what came before but to steer where I choose to go. The world is wide, and we only have so many days to spend exploring. Given druthers, I turn south again and again.

—SANDRA BEASLEY

There are many Souths. You wouldn't think southern Illinois is one of them, but it's close enough, more or less Appalachia with a shade of "midwestern" reticence, silos, and soybeans. For me it's speech and food, and sometimes flags. My college girlfriend was from Chicago, and one night, in a bookstore, an actress friend of hers repeated back to me the way I said "theater." "*Thee-ay*-ter," she said, drawing out the long "a." That's when I knew. My ancestors migrated in a sort of retrograde orbit: Scotland — Tennessee — Ozarks — Illinois, and you can hear the residue when my grandfather says "a-goin'." *I'm give out. She's all swelled up you guys didn't take your boots off. He come up here the other day.* Also, try to explain biscuits and gravy or fried carp to a northerner. Also, I count four Confederate flags when I drive home from Indiana.

—PAUL BONE

I'm white and, like both my parents, was born and raised in the Deep South. But they became academics, shedding their accents and reshaping themselves against their histories, and my childhood friends were a motley group whose histories mostly lay elsewhere. I grew up, then, feeling foreign in my native land. I looked for seams (and semes) that separated and stitched together a layered history—some visible (Apalachee middens, Spanish forts, antebellum plantations, Confederate flags), others audible. Native and European languages jockeyed for naming rights ("Tallahassee" is from the Apalachee, "Florida" from the Spanish), and words told stories, although sometimes you had to scratch the surface of English to hear them: "St. Marks" had been "San Marcos," and every alligator there was *"el lagarto."* Maybe such confluences helped make me a writer; certainly they made the South, my relation to it, and its relation to America inescapable subjects for me.

—GEOFFREY BROCK

The South, to me, is an elegant subterfuge. It is a fig leaf of manners hiding an atavistic, bestial appetite. It is the whiskey-fueled howl around the ancestral fire and it is a strict and measured cotillion, as well, the rouged and powdered faces twisted into a rictus beneath the gibbous September moon. The South is a copperhead coiled in the blackberry brambles where a child leans down to pluck the plumpest clusters. It is the grimace behind the mask of gentle mirth, the seductive evasion meant to conceal and confound. The South is the gorgeous lie one wants most to believe, the old men who told it in rolled-up shirt sleeves summer after summer, and the boy I was still straining to listen and remember, who tells it now, but tells it slant, if only to get it right and say it true.

—MORRI CREECH

To expand on a comment I once made regarding my native state of Kentucky: poetry in the South (in general) is still about something. In a post-post-modern age that has seen our politics, culture, and system of social valuation become more and more unmoored from the tangible, tactile, olfactory, etc. reality of embodied experience, Southern poetry (in general) tends to remain true to its Romanticist history and potential of accounting for, and to, real lives, groping to find real meaning that is grounded in the (sometimes frustratingly) undeniable physical it-ness of the world we inhabit. And therein lies its grand, expansive, blooming, buzzing multiplicity and diversity. Like a vast, vibrant cultural seed bank, Southern poetry (in general) continues to retrieve and preserve modes of experience, meaning, relationship that, however diffuse or different, bind us together in a shared struggle to discover and affirm our common humanity in a shared world.

—TONY CRUNK

In *Democratic Vistas* (1871), Walt Whitman envisioned "the traits of America" in the aftermath of the Civil War as forming a composite "giant growth," one blending characteristics of the North, West, and South. From the North would come "intellect, the sun of all things," along with "the idea of unswayable justice." The West would contribute "solid personality, with blood and brawn, and the deep quality of all-accepting fusion." And the South? "From the south the living soul, the animus of good and bad, haughtily admitting no demonstration but its own." Nearly 150 years later, Whitman's psychic geography may feel quaint or obsolete. But as a native New Englander who has been to all fifty states and lived in Virginia for the last thirty-five years, I recognize something corresponding roughly to the boundaries of what Whitman knew as the South, something with a vigorous living soul, complex, diverse, divided, animated by good and bad, and, yes, *haughty*, from a root that meant to nourish or grow.

— STEPHEN CUSHMAN

As time advances and history deepens, the term "Southern" gets all the more slippery—almost to the point of being unsustainable, or unsustainable in its simplicity. Can Southern be "Dixie" and blk? Can it be Queer and Baptist? Muslim and pork-forward? Yes, of course, but not in a way that is comfortable, not in a way that makes an easy flag. My people are from South Carolina (Darlington / Columbia) and Virginia (Lynchburg), but northern Virginia adjacent to Washington, DC, where I live, looks nothing like those traditionally "Southern" environments. And that matters because the South, maybe more than any other region of America, is invested in maintaining its "purity" in regard to the character of its early settlement. But even that change is truly Southern, as the South remains a site for arrival—but for Latinx and Asian immigrants now. I don't think I'll ever feel any ownership of southernness, but it passes through me and I through it.

— KYLE DARGAN

I had never stepped foot in the South before taking my present teaching job. The fact that I'm still here after fifteen years would, then, probably suggest that it's not that bad. And I suppose that, to me and many of my friends in the academy, that's a rather typical response: *it's not that bad*. But that's not the most ringing of endorsements, and it doesn't gesture at what's good—really good—about the South. The South is about as fecund a place as I have ever experienced. Everything grows, especially the things we don't want to grow. Everything comes inside in the summer, especially the things we don't want inside. There's a kind of ecstatic excess here—in the extraordinary growing season, in the atrociously fatty "traditional" cuisine, in the by turns mellifluous and twangy speech. The South is like other places I've lived, true, only more so. How can all of that be bad for poetry?

—CHAD DAVIDSON

The South is the beast that lives inside the minds of its writers. It is an idea, a burden, a shadow that follows us no matter how far away we may flee. The Southern poet has a sensuous relationship to the land—at times exquisite and feral in its beauty, other times suddenly violent and hostile. This is true of its people as well, and it seems to write about the South is to try to reconcile oneself with that appetite for violence and cruelty, as well as the fierce love for one's roots, that we hold deep in the bones. The poet is born out of wrestling with the history of her land and her place in it.

—ANSEL ELKINS

Today I was reading Maggie Nelson's *The Argonauts* and came to a passage in which she discusses Anne Carson, during a lecture, introducing the concept new to Nelson, "leaving a space empty so that God could rush in." What's Southern poetry? It's reading Nelson reading Carson—these contemporary intellects who perceive the abstract and universal—and feeling part of the conversation. But it's also recognizing that "southern" isn't universal, isn't the default, but set apart as "other." And that can be a strength, too. It's the other that's mysterious, textured, not tapped-out. I love New York but don't want to contribute to the world another poem about how hard it is to find a parking space in Brooklyn. And as for

Nelson and Carson—they have super big and fascinating brains, but, well, damn, everyone in Mississippi who ever slow danced at junior prom has been told a dozen times to leave room for Jesus.

—BETH ANN FENNELLY

I have now lived the majority of my writing life in the South, and my adopted geography has profoundly shaped my outlook. My reading now includes Southern poets and their ideas of what a poem should be and do. My writing would not be what it is without James Dickey, Betty Adcock, David Bottoms, Claudia Emerson, etc. The South has also led me to deepen my connections to the land. I cut my teeth in the rush and teem of Philadelphia and New York City. But my later years have unfolded near bayous and muddy lakes, among live oaks and loblolly pines. My lungs have learned to absorb the ferocious humidity. An armadillo might crawl now, a catfish slide, into one of my dreams. My ears have attuned to all sorts of drawls—from the mechanic who bemoans the over-engineering of today's cars, from bellowing cows I pass while driving my kids to school.

—GREG FRASER

A home long before the colony was lost, the South sings the blues. Every day, blue is in the mountain ridge, the laws, the collars, the grass. Blue means certain hounds and hydrangeas, painted porch ceilings, and a special Carolina shade, wide and clear above the coastlines. Blue is in the plate specials and the hickory smoke of barbecue pits. Sometimes it is hotter than blue blazes. Sometimes folks make off-color remarks. Blue is how some people feel in gerrymandered voting districts. White folks might say *I don't care if they're black, white or blue,* forgetting the combination that makes a bruise. Stuck in city sprawl, we Southerners are fixin' to. Even when we feel blue, we're neighborly. We hold the door and smile.

—JULIE FUNDERBURK

The South makes me flinch. Occasionally, the South makes me proud. When my neighbors in western New York mention it, I tense, ready to defend it. Every year I host a Mardi Gras party, also known as my Yankee Outreach party; I simmer giant pots of gumbo and try to convince my guests that okra isn't slimy. The South is heat and cicadas, blacktop and red clay, football and "all y'all," bigotry served with a smile. In Rome on New Year's Day, I cooked black-eyed peas, broccoli rabe, and biscuits with *latte intero* and yogurt substituted for buttermilk. The South is its people, some of whom scare me, many of whom I love. Southern poetry encompasses all of these contradictions, embraces them, explores them, laughs at them, tries to make sense of them. I carry its rhythms with me everywhere.

—JULIANA GRAY

Our understanding of southern poetry is a moving target—just like our understanding of the South. Technically, southern poetry would be poetry written by someone living in the South. However, some poets seem especially to have "southern" voices. Andrew Hudgins would be a good example. Dave Smith. Ellen Bryant Voigt. Yusef Komunyakaa. Natasha Trethewey. The work of these writers returns regularly to southern figures / issues: the heat, the Civil War, racial tension, live oaks, enormous roaches, kudzu . . . . Still, what we think of as southern is changing rapidly in part because of the growth and continued diversification of big cities like Atlanta and Houston. I am a northern transplant, but the South—its beauty and its troubles—has infected my work as it seems to anyone who lives south of the Mason–Dixon Line long enough. I am excited to appear in an anthology that reflects the growing complexity.

—BETH GYLYS

Although I was born in New Orleans, I moved around because my father was in the Air Force. From ten to eighteen I lived in Honolulu, but both of my parents were from the South, and my mother especially had a huge fund of Southernisms spiked with hard-line biblical admonishments, such as "Vengeance is mine, sayeth the Lord" and "Vanity, vanity, all is vanity." It drove me crazy, but now I look back on her lingo with such fondness. I married a man from Louisiana, and his mother added her sayings: "He's as crazy as a rat in a coffee can" and "He has less sense than God gave a billy goat." Language is God in the Deep South.

—BARBARA HAMBY

The search for authenticity (e.g., the search for an authentic, singularly identifiable South) is probably a fool's errand. To be definitive is to be ridiculous. Say something inane like, "The South is barbecue and football," and I say, "The South is a myth perpetuated by the status quo." Say something highfalutin like, "The South is a myth perpetuated by the status quo," and I invite you to my tailgate. So, if we can't define it, does it exist? For me, The South, like the self, remains an *it*. Theorists deny it, but one intuits: It's there. (Here?) Thus, I do assign it distinctive qualities, my favorite of which is its language. I often listen with wonder when Southerners speak. And, for me, all language is most wondrous as poetry. So why would a Southern poetry, if it can make such sound, not make sense?

—HASTINGS HENSEL

The South falls between a set of latitudes and longitudes, man-imagined lines on a map. It's a set of parameters, a storied space. The South is where my long-lived great-grandfather started his third family with a woman about half his age. It's where his father (whose mother and father were from the South) was born in 1812. The South's regional certainty seems to be born out of a war over an economy borne up by slave labor. Born in 1856, my great-grandfather was once considered property. The South is that history and what's to come—that is, longitudinally speaking the South has changed, is changing. The South is storied; it's the land and the way that shapes our tongues. Since poetry is a linguistic exploration or an articulation of the worlds we live in or aspire to, then Southern Poetry is those speech acts composed by tongues informed by the land and all that forever happens here.

—SEAN HILL

The American South is about return. Born in Austin, Texas, I grew up Palestinian in the Middle East. When I returned to America, it was in Georgia that I first implemented my belonging, my nationalism. In the AAA of the Peach State (Athens, Atlanta, Augusta), something in me connected *the southerner* to *the global south.* Specifically, it was Black presence and culture to which I related on historical and linguistic grounds. The latter has to do with my travels between formal and colloquial Arabic in its particular "southern" Palestinian accent (as spoken in Isdud, my ancestral village, which is now erased). The American South, despite the "patriotic wreaths" laid at its quarantine into a regional phenomenon, remains an All-American aesthetic. An aesthetic of erasure, camouflage, magnolias, sweet onions, and regeneration. Always the "again." Who are you that stands in the contrapuntal line of arrival? A veil across the stars.

—FADY JOUDAH

In college, I worked with a former football player from Hammond, Louisiana, named Clarence. Clarence made some of the best gumbo I've ever eaten. When I asked him for the recipe, he told me it wasn't written down, just a family tradition passed along. A couple of nights later, Clarence told me a story about his great-great-grandfather, a cook on a river boat. His grandfather had been on a long trip and wanted to make something really special for his wife's dinner but all he had was a little flour, some butter, and three onions. Over the course of the shift, Clarence relayed how, stop by stop, his grandfather swapped, traded, sweet talked and beguiled all the ingredients for his gumbo. To me, southern poetry is like Clarence's story: a long, rambling, and ever-changing collection of disparate characters and landscapes that come together to form, like Clarence's gumbo, something beautiful and new.

—TERRY KENNEDY

"I dont! I dont hate it! I dont hate it!" So, Quentin Compson. I have lived below the Georgia–Florida border for the past thirty-five years, in the South but never of it. Donald Justice lived more than half his life north of the Mason–Dixon and west of the Mississippi but never stopped being a Southerner. I will never be more than a cast-iron Yankee, although I lived in New England little more than a decade. (I've spent longer in England than New England.) It's curious, these identities bred and born, later borne as well. I don't feel responsible for the South, antebellum or post-; but any mode of analysis so close to the bone demands a measure of shame for its slight freedom, and a measure of guilt for having taken an inheritance by theft.

—WILLIAM LOGAN

Considering "southern poetry" as a category goes back at least to the April 1922 issue of *Poetry*, which included a survey called "Poetry South." While the authors, DuBose Heyward and Hervey Allen, generally approved of the poetry coming from the region, they also acknowledged familiar barriers. I grew up fully aware of these realities, ingrained limitations in the South based on race, class, geography, and opportunity. I would like to think our poets of the region have found some way—whether through sheer invention or political liberation or the slow passage of time—to rise above these old limits on thought and feeling and originality. My hope is we have something to say together. But, of course, anything to do with the South is more complicated than this. It's an ongoing endeavor, and that larger endeavor is always what poetry is for.

—MAURICE MANNING

As a reader, for me it begins with Dickey, advances with Robert Morgan, Jim Wayne Miller, and Fred Chappell, and slowly opens up to include a wider range (women, writers of color, millennials) as I grow into and with the scene, which I don't really see in terms of region. Maybe because I am a northerner at heart, or that I moved around most of my life, I don't see things in relation to the Mason–Dixon Line (or, as my buddy Keith Flynn calls it, the "Manson–Nixon Line").

—SEBASTIAN MATTHEWS

Although I've lived in the South nearly half my life, I'm still very much an outsider and thus a little wary of defining it or its poetry. I'll say this, though: one thing I admire about southern poetry is its resistance—maybe it's an immunity—to some of the trendier poetic movements. Narrative poetry, of course, isn't eyed suspiciously here, while clarity and precision never seem to go out of style. The South hardly has an exclusive claim on clarity, but clarity certainly seems to matter more here than it does elsewhere, and when I think about my favorite southern poets—David Bottoms, Claudia Emerson, Natasha Trethewey—I see that they all seek to clarify, rather than obscure, the world.

—JAMES MAY

A chile said *What is the South?* How could I answer the chile? I do not know what it is any more than she. I fear it must be the flag of my disposition, out of shameful white stuff woven. And I protest with Quentin Compson, *I dont hate it! I dont hate it!* And the chile asked me *What is Southern poetry?* I said to the chile it is *pine cones and corn pones*, a darling I once murdered. Too Southern, too "Southern," too *too*, like the South. Can I permit Spanish moss in a poem? Can I permit a glass of sweet tea? I confess my abiding love of sweet tea, someone bring me a glass right now. *Thank you, Sugar.* My favorite Southern poet is Walt Whitman. He never needs to say *I dont hate it!* And neither do I. Do I contradict myself? All right then.

—BRENT NEWSOM

I carry two ideas of the South in my mind—one the mythic, nostalgic, and inevitably *white* version with which I was raised, and the other the region as it really is: multiracial, endlessly complex, and forever marked by slavery, Jim Crow, and the horrors of the lynching epidemic. Now that I have spent years researching the history of white terrorism in my home-place of Forsyth County, Georgia, it is impossible for me to ever go back to celebrating "the old South." It's not that I don't still sometimes pine for the beloved Georgia foothills of my childhood. But I know now that the agrarian idyll is and always has been a lie, which erases centuries of labor by people of color. So what does that leave me to love as a native son? Not the imaginary but the actual South. The whole haunted, and haunting, mess of it.

—PATRICK PHILLIPS

The land I know best is now called Abbeville County, South Carolina. Before I knew what people call it, and before I didn't know and just had the feeling of it in my body, it had other names. I use these ones so you'll recognize it, at least on a map. But better to start there, by the creek, by the tulip poplar growing next to the culvert that used to be a wooden bridge I swung my feet off of that used to be air. Better to begin with the feel of air on my face, of petals, leaves. I can see now some of the sorrow of so many people denied a place, the generations of thefts that allowed me, middle-class white kid, to get acquainted with this landscape. How do you hold a love for the land grown over years, and an awareness that the love has come at the cost of others' lives and livelihoods?

—ANNA LENA PHILLIPS BELL

A circuit-riding priest named my part of the South *Côte Blanche*, a blur of white-washed shotgun houses along Bayou Lafourche near Louisiana's delta. The Cajun Coast, made up of Acadians, Italians, Irish, German, Creoles, native peoples, and others, is as paradoxical as the swamp: hospitable and clannish, devoutly Catholic and doctrinally ambivalent, attached to the land and in denial about its disappearance. The Religion of the Lost Cause is mostly lost on my neighbors, who live in the present tense of food, family, and feast days, with contributions from all ethnicities. Living rituals associated with religion and agriculture—Mass and Mardi Gras—perpetuate identity more than politics do. Time is registered by major hurricanes. My home, not wholly removed from its Southern neighbors to the east and north, is an indigenous culture created by people who had been marginalized elsewhere, a deep, dense swamp of very different people who assimilated to the *land*, not primarily to a dominant group, enabling a more accessible sense of belonging.

—MARTHA SERPAS

When people ask, "Where are you from?" they are really asking where you were born. "Not here. Up North." But if I spent the second half of my childhood in the marshlands of Florida sixty-eight miles east of where my husband was born, am I a Southerner? It took me two decades into my life to taste the bitter bite of collards and black-eyed peas, side of cornbread sopping up the potlikker, on New Year's Day. My husband, my daughter, born on Peachtree Road, both Southerners. Me? My grandparents boarded separate ships from Ireland pointed toward the same coordinates 218 miles north of the Mason–Dixon. Down here the magnolia trees never cease to amaze me. The long ropes of their roots sprawling across yards, until the canopy becomes a lost thought, and then the petals' slow unfolding each May, my birth month, yielding a prehistoric scent, whispering, "We've been here long before any of you."

—MEGAN SEXTON

The poetry of the South has a history as complicated as the South itself. I only want to say here that Southern poetry includes more than the Fugitives and Agrarians—or that lingering ghost of the New Criticism. In my experience, these schools are often the only traditions mentioned when discussing Southern poetry, but people have been singing in the South for as long as there have been people in the South. That music is rich and diverse, even if most anthologies would have it otherwise. There is a lot to be learned from the Fugitives, of course, but we are all diminished if we also don't look past them. It would be a mistake to assume that all Southern poets writing today are descendants of Warren, Tate, and Ransom. The talents of the South are sprawling like the landscapes they were / are born into—in all their manifestations.

—MICHAEL SHEWMAKER

The South is to blame for my prom dresses, but it gets credit for my accent. The South is to blame for my long-winded emails, but it gets credit for my efforts to be polite. The South is to blame for my former ignorance of Asian cuisines, but it gets credit for my firsthand knowledge of farm animals. The South is to blame for my poetry's biblical references, but it gets credit for my faith in the musicality of language.

—EVIE SHOCKLEY

"South" has always meant, to me, "Other," which may be why I love it. Although I've now lived south of the Mason–Dixon Line much, much longer than I lived above it, I'm still struck, decades later, by its linguistic and geographic vernacular, its orality, its fecundity. Southerners (themselves manifold, diverse, polarized) may find my catalog cliché, but to someone raised in a place with real, long winters and a certain surly communal restraint, the paradoxes of the South are far from patent, easily caricatured, or one-dimensional. They are both familiar and strange. The (in)toxic(ating) perfume of any magnolia and honeysuckle-suffused Virginia night in June, for instance, always has a Road to Damascus effect on me, something that I'm sure has contributed to the opulence of my own baroque poetics. Never quite at home here, I all the better see myself and my way. For that I'm abidingly indebted, as a poet, as a person.

—LISA RUSS SPAAR

It was years spent away from the South (in London and Oxford) that convinced me that I was Southern after all. Returning to live in Athens and then Atlanta, I became aware of a strain of Southern literature that wasn't shy about literary allusion or technical verve. I stumbled on Turner Cassity's styptic, well-traveled, urbane verses and wrote to him. I lived in John Crowe Ransom's niece's basement. James Dickey was legendary for alcohol-soaked anecdotes, but *The Early Motion* made old cadences new. I am still attracted to poets associated with my hometown—I admire the work of Natasha Trethewey, her way with myth and tradition, clear-eyed, unsentimental. My poems contain kudzu, roadkill, arrowhead hunting, fishing, and mason jars, but also classical myth and traditional meter. I have lived more than half my adult life not in Athens, Georgia, but Athens, Greece. Moving to Greece does not make me a Greek poet, but leaving the South might make me a Southern one.

—A. E. STALLINGS

The summers so sticky that a shovel almost seems to stand on its own in the humidity, Alabama clay smeared along every tire coming out of the woods, its distinct orange on every welcome mat at our front doors; Decoration Day, when we sit on the graves of our kin and tell their stories, which are now our stories, eating fried chicken thighs, gizzards, livers, hearts, collards, snap beans, butterbeans cooked down so soft a baby can manage them, Johnny cakes (*not* sweet), saving all the sugar for the tea; the crappie spawning in blowdowns we seek when native azaleas strike the banks with fiery blooms in spring; bayberry, wax myrtle, croton, Cahaba lily, Alabama snow wreath and the invasives: the mimosa's pink pappus, the wisteria and kudzu—how they climb the trees, strangle them—their purple flowers like grape clusters, the oakleaf hydrangea's teardrop.

—ADAM VINES

Having lived and traveled extensively throughout the United States, I've observed that from town to town, there are few differences between the north and south beyond the landscape and weather. Most people have the same concerns about family, education, life stability, taxes—and in general, the norms and mores remain the same one place to the next. The big southern city is not much more than big corporations vying for everyone's greenbacks, just like northern cities. Most businesses are chains. The real South is when you travel thirty miles outside any metro area. In Flannery O'Connor's *Wise Blood*, Enoch Emery proclaimed that in Taulkinham the people are not friendly. That's the truth to a degree, but what O'Connor was really saying is that in a small town everyone is friendly, to a point of being nosy. The South is good weather, nice people, and rural peacefulness when I want it.

—WILLIAM WALSH

In the South, the idea of place is everything, but even in the works by poets whom I think of as distinctly "Southern" there are contraries. Is Dickey's South the river that don't go to Aintry, or is it the blue windows of Piedmont Hospital, where his father lies above the snarl of Atlanta traffic? The answer of course is both, suggesting that the bifurcated South of the Snopeses and the Sartorises repeats itself in the collision of the rural and the urban that is my own home state of Georgia. That sense of place, of its deep attachment to a past that isn't even past, is lacking in my own writing, I think. My landscapes tend to be psychological, and my sense of history or at least my attention to that sense works itself out in spots of time, not contours.

—THEODORE WOROZBYT

The South is where Spanish moss and wisteria, river banks and menace creep across my poems if unchecked. Where I grew up without a drawl in Atlanta, envious of the music of accents beyond the city limits. Where once in college I looked up from a brunch menu, blinking, when a friend fumed at the "Old Plantation Breakfast Skillet." Where I recall her anger at that grotesque nostalgia now as I shift uncomfortably on a folding chair at a wedding, notes of Pachelbel's Canon drifting across the plantation lawn as the bride approaches in a horse-drawn carriage and I try to reconcile the charm of this landscape with its brutal history.

—JOSEPHINE YU

Attributions

NOTE: For all poems appearing in this volume, if permission to reprint was needed, credit information is provided below. If no credit information for a poem appears below, permission to publish in this volume was granted by the individual poet.

Beasley, Sandra. "Halloween" and "The Wake" from *Count the Waves: Poems* by Sandra Beasley. Copyright © 2015 by Sandra Beasley. Used by permission of W.W. Norton & Company, Inc.

Belieu, Erin. "How We Count in the South" and "When at a Certain Party in NYC" from *Slant Six* (2014). Copper Canyon Press.

Brown, Jericho. "The Tradition" and "Foreday in the Morning" from *The Tradition*. Copyright © 2019 by Jericho Brown. Reprinted with the permission of The Permissions Company, LLC on behalf of Copper Canyon Press, coppercanyonpress.org.

Dargan, Kyle. "The Wandered" from *Logorrhea Dementia* and "Notice to the Addict" from *Bouquet of Hungers*, University of Georgia Press.

Elkins, Ansel. "Blues for the Death of the Sun" and "Going to the Movies Alone" from *Blue Yodel* (2015). Used by permission of Yale University Press.

Fennelly, Beth Ann. "Bite Me" from *Tender Hooks: Poems,* copyright 2004 by Beth Ann Fennelly. Used by permission of W.W. Norton & Company, Inc. "First Warm Day in a College Town" from *Unmentionables: Poems* by Beth Ann Fennelly. Copyright © 2008 by Beth Ann Fennelly. Used by permission of W.W. Norton & Company, Inc.

Fraser, Gregory. "The Theft" and "Not a Word" from *Destined for*

Flight. Evanston, IL: Northwestern University Press, 2014.

Graham, Natalie J. "In the Beginning, Death" and "Intersections" from *Begin with a Failed Body*, University of Georgia Press.

Hayes, Terrance. "The Avocado" and "God Is an American" from *Lighthead: Poems*, copyright © 2010 by Terrance Hayes. Used by permission of Penguin Books, an imprint of Penguin Publishing Group, a division of Penguin Random House LLC. All rights reserved.

Hill, Sean. "Boy" and "Milledgeville Haibun" from *Blood Ties & Brown Liquor*, University of Georgia Press.

Joudah, Fady. "The Way Back" from *The Earth in the Attic* (2008). Used by permission of Yale University Press.

Meitner, Erika. "Wal*Mart Supercenter" and "In/exhaustible" from *Copia*. Copyright © 2014 by Erika Meitner. Reprinted with the permission of The Permissions Company, LLC on behalf of BOA Editions, Ltd., boaeditions.org. All rights reserved.

Newsom, Brent. "Pfc. Mason Buxton Embraces the Suck" and "Moonrise" from *Love's Labors*. Copyright © 2015 by Brent Newsom. Reprinted with the permission of The Permissions Company, LLC on behalf of CavanKerry Press, Ltd., www.cavankerry.org. All rights reserved.

Phillips Bell, Anna Lena. "Midafternoon" and "Hush" from *Ornament* (2017). Used with permission from University of North Texas Press.

Rathburn, Chelsea. "English Sonnet" from *A Raft of Grief*. Copyright © 2013 by Chelsea Rathburn. Reprinted with the permission of The Permissions Company, LLC on behalf of Autumn House Press, www.autumnhouse.org.

Serpas, Martha. "Poem Found" and "The Water" from *The Dirty*

Acknowledgments

My gratitude to those who were instrumental (with encouragement, support, knowledge, kindness, criticism) in helping bring this anthology to light: Chad Abushanab, Courtney Burkholder, Chad Davidson, Greg Fraser, Bryan Giemza, Paul Hunton, Meghan Poch, Lisa Russ Spaar, Brian Still, Peter Vertacnik, Adam Vines, The Sewanee Writers Conference, Virginia Center for the Creative Arts. A development leave and other extraordinary assistance from Texas Tech University contributed to the making of this book. Todd Murphy, beautiful maker, fellow Southerner, I send heavenward my thanks for the amazing cover image. You are sorely missed.

About the Editor

John Poch's poems have appeared in *Poetry, Paris Review, Yale Review, The Nation*, and other magazines. In 2019, he published two collections of poems: *Texases* (WordFarm) and *Between Two Rivers* (TTU Press). He is President's Excellence Research Professor in the English department at Texas Tech University.